Character Assassination

Ray Alan Collins

Character Assassination

ISBN 978-0-9844818-6-6

This book is dedicated to my father and my friend, Austin L. Collins, who taught me the love of writing, the love of mysteries, and the love of people.

Acknowledgments

There are contributors to this work who merit acknowledgment and heartfelt thanks.

The patience, encouragement, and continual support of my loving wife, Darlene, is at the top of the list. Without her, you would not be reading these words. She has not only been supportive in the background, she has been my greatest critic and editor. I gripe at her when she asks the hard questions, yet I love her for doing so. It is only through her that I can see what the reader sees.

Thank you, Darlene.

Through my entire writing career, I've had teenagers at home. They too have been patient and loving with my absence and exhaustion

Thank you, Melissa, Lucinda, Leslie, Crystal, Sharlotte, Roslynd, and Adrian.

Table of Contents

Chapter 1

Where there is injustice and frustration, the potentialities for violence are greater

~Martin Luther King

The doorbell had rung twice. Then some persistent fool started hammering on the door. Damn! It was 8:30 am. This might be morning for some; it was the middle of my night. I remember thinking, "Either someone is dead or someone's going to be."

I got off the bed. I hadn't really gotten into it the night before. I'd worked till dawn and done some really good writing. I remembered putting up the Scotch and setting the timer on the coffee pot then just falling onto the bed.

I started for the stairs wearing just my jeans. My mother would have chastised me for answering the door while I was "indecent," but this person was now alternately hammering on the door and ringing the doorbell. At the head of the stairs, I picked up my revolver and stuck it in my waistband at the small of my back.

"Keep your pants on!" I thundered as I got to the bottom of the stairs.

The hammering stopped.

In the foyer, I turned off the security system and opened the door. Outside stood a blond woman in a green business suit. The suit consisted of a knee-length skirt and a blazer. She wore a white blouse and a narrow tie of the same green material as the blazer. She had on a pair of black flats to complete the wardrobe.

This woman was about five feet six inches tall. Her hair was neck length and cut page-boy style. In her right hand was a very expensive-looking briefcase and in her left was a black shoulder bag. There were beads of perspiration on her lip. Overall, she looked pretty plain-Jane, except for the briefcase and the stretch limo at the curb.

"It takes you long enough to answer the door," she complained. "Are you Tip Thinn?"

The question startled me. Tip Thinn is the pen name I'd used for my recent mystery novels. As far as I knew, nobody in San Antonio knew the name except, maybe, my ex-wife. This woman certainly didn't look like anyone who would be a friend of Harriet's.

"No, lady, my name's not Thinn, but my patience is. You've got the wrong house and you're interrupting my sleep." I started to push the door closed, but she stepped forward.

"Very well, Mr. Noble. I've got some business to discuss with you."

Now I was even more startled. Whoever this woman was, she knew my name, my pen name, and my address. I was a little intrigued, but I was also "indecent", armed, and very tired. "Lady, I don't discuss business in the middle of the night with people I don't even know. Go away!"

"Charles Stonemason, in New York, said you're a very good writer and a pretty good businessman." She stood, unmoving, in my doorway.

"Okay, lady, you've done your homework. You know who I am, what I do, and you know who my agent is. But, you don't seem to understand this is the middle of my night. I'm tired and I'm going to bed. Care to join me?"

"Don't flatter yourself, Mr. Noble. I'll leave now and be back at noon to discuss business. Please be dressed and you won't need the gun." She turned and started down the walk.

"I'll still be asleep at noon!" I yelled at her. She had my interest up. I hated to admit it, but she did. I had tried to embarrass her with the going-to-bed comment so she would leave. She hadn't even blinked.

"I'll be ready at two," I yelled at her as she got into the limo. I watched the long, white car pull out of sight before I grabbed the phone. That damned agent of mine had some questions to answer.

"I'm sorry, Mr. Noble, Mr. Stonemason is out of the office and I don't know how to reach him or when he'll return." I'd met Chucky Stonemason's secretary a couple of times. She was a sweet old lady, super at her job. She had one serious failing - she couldn't lie worth a damn.

"Mrs. Cooper, I know you're being paid to lie to me, so I'm not going to be mad at you." She started to protest but I cut her off, "Tell Chucky I'm mad at him and he'd better call me within the hour!"

"I'll give Mr. Stonemason the message as soon as he returns, Mr. Noble." She was patient and really tried to do as she had been told.

"Thank you, Mrs. Cooper." I hung up the phone and headed back to bed.

Charles Stonemason, Chucky to his best clients, was a man who thrived on information. He had a phone in his car, one in his boat and one in every room in his house. And with all of that, he carried a cellular! His business revolved around being in touch, around having information. If he cheated on his wife, I doubt the thought of cheating on Mrs. Stonemason had ever occurred to him, but if he did, he'd still leave a number where he could be reached. I didn't believe for a minute he was beyond the reach of Mrs. Cooper.

Chucky has always known I'm somewhat of a recluse. And I'm pretty sure that this woman with the limo knew how and where to find me because Chucky had told her. I was even more sure since he was avoiding me.

As I laid down on the bed, still furious at Chucky, a sudden thought came to me. That woman, I didn't even know her name, couldn't have seen the gun. How did she know? Had she guessed? Had Chucky warned her? Damn!

An hour later I was still awake tossing and turning on the bed; I was still aggravated. That woman had pushed her way into my life, or at least into my privacy. I hate when people take advantage of my time or my personal life. People always complicate life. I'm not really a recluse - I'm a hermit.

I was also furious at myself. I despise manipulative women and I'd let this one manipulate me. I gave up on the sleep I both needed and wanted. I tried to call Chucky again but Mrs. Cooper still stood by her story. I hung up and called FTD and sent Mrs. Cooper some flowers. She seemed to be the only loyal human being I knew.

I needed a hot shower ... now!

Chapter 2

A man always has two reasons for what he does — a good one, and the real one.

~*J. Pierpont Morgan*

The grandfather clock in the hall started chiming two o'clock at the same time the doorbell started ringing. I still hadn't heard from Chucky. I'd had a shower, breakfast and finally a shot of Scotch to calm down.

I've heard that there are some writers who aren't temperamental. In fact, my ex-wife used to bleat at me all the time about those mythical beasts. Her lawyer said I wasn't temperamental - just spoiled. I don't know if either one of them was right, but I like my privacy and my work.

I opened the door and Miss Greensuit just came right on in. She still had the expensive briefcase but this time the limo was pulling away. "I hope you can recall that thing," I said sarcastically. "You don't look like you're built for taxi cabs."

She didn't reply; she simply started for the dining room. I caught her elbow and headed her toward the living room. "We'll discuss whatever business you think we have in there!" I told her.

"The table would be better for work," she countered as she stopped.

"We aren't going to work. We're going to discuss." I nudged her toward the living room. "Have a seat on the sofa. The coffee's hot; would you care for some?"

She replied icily, "We're going to discuss not drink coffee."

"I never discuss anything without coffee." I'd offered her some because my mother had taught me to be courteous to my guests. But this woman was irritating.

As she moved into the living room, I went to the kitchen. I had to smile inwardly as I poured my coffee. We'd been sparing with power plays and she was pretty good. But she'd decided to beard the lion in his den and this lion had a few tricks in store for her. First of all, that sofa had a very weak spring - it wasn't much better than sitting on the floor. The kids love it and call it a ride, which is why I keep it. Whenever someone sat on it, they sank and their knees were about chest high. The coffee table was too close for anyone to stretch their legs out in front of them, so I figured she'd be mighty uncomfortable sitting there in her knee length skirt. On the other side of the coffee table was my massive recliner. I'd be like a king on a throne!

Since she said she didn't come to drink coffee, I took only one cup and felt very smug about myself until I found her sitting in my recliner. Damn, she was good!

I wanted to strangle her, but recovered my composure quickly and walked to the fireplace. I put my cup on the mantle, leaned on my elbow, and asked, "Now, Miss Whatever-your-name-is, what do we have to discuss?"

From where she sat, she had to turn to face me. I could see the irritation in her eyes, but there was none in her voice. "My name is Diana Faire and I have a writing offer to discuss with you."

I waited for her to continue. When she didn't, I started to tell her she'd have to find someone else to write her life story. Just as I started to speak, she asked, "Who are your favorite authors?"

Damn, she was good! She'd waited me out and then cut me off just before I spoke. Irritated, I replied, "What does that have to do with our business? Are you offering me an assignment or trying to find someone better?"

"Mr. Noble, it's two-fifteen." She was speaking calmly, with none of the edge to her voice. She seemed almost friendly as she continued, "We've spent a quarter of an hour fencing and taking verbal shots at each other. I have a unique and interesting proposal for you. I'm pretty sure you're the writer I want but this assignment is extremely important to me. I must be absolutely sure. I know you've had kind of a slump since your divorce..."

I started to protest but she waved me off. Her green eyes showed genuine concern. "I mean no offense; I've read everything you've had published. Your westerns are superb. I thrilled at your poetry. I don't have much interest in children's books but I enjoyed yours. You're very versatile, Mr. Noble."

She was speaking with an affection that was almost sensual. It was a little spooky and I didn't know where it was leading, but she was sincere and had struck my vanity. I'd heard of writers who didn't have enlarged egos, but I wasn't one of them. She had things to say that I wanted to hear. She was sort of an animated fan letter. I decided to hear her out just for the compliments if nothing else.

If she was going to gush out her praise, I was going to listen - but not standing at the mantle. We might as well both be comfortable. "Are you sure you wouldn't you care for some coffee, Miss Faire?"

"Mrs. Faire," she corrected. "With one sugar, please."

This whole thing seemed to be getting very weird or at least taking a very unexpected turn. I got her coffee and found myself wondering what kind of unique and interesting deal she was going to offer.

With our coffee, we moved to the dining room table. We talked of authors and literature, of styles and stories. It was past six-thirty when she again asked about my favorite writers.

"Diana, there are so many wonderful writers and so many classes of literature, I just don't know where to begin."

"Begin with the classics," she suggested.

"Robert Lewis Stevenson, of course. Shakespeare is required reading if you are to consider yourself an educated person, but his Elizabethan English is tough."

She asked next of mystery writers.

"Agatha Christie, Sir Arthur Conan-Doyle, and, of course, Poe. He is closer to suspense than mystery, I guess. Although *Murders in the Rue Morgue* was the world's first detective mystery."

She said, "Poe is closer to macabre. What about Stephen King?"

"I never developed an interest in his stuff. He's very vivid and has an awesome imagination, but ..."

You write Westerns," she continued. "Who are your favorite writers in your particular field? There must be quite a few."

"Zane Grey. He's one of my favorites. L'Amour, too. His action's faster but Grey is more picturesque. Luke Short is good. Tabor Evans is alright but the whole concept of "Adult Westerns" sort of bothers me. Those books are sold mostly on a few sex scenes added to a feeble plot. And the sex scenes seem to be there for sensationalism rather than to develop the plot. Those books also tend to stray from the true Cowboy ethic - from the moral values of the era. I know people had sex back then, like now, and there was prostitution and everything, but the way the Adult Westerns portray things doesn't fit with what I believe."

I hesitated. "Diana, there are just so many. I really don't know who's best. Why the interest in who I like?"

"What about Davy Hoyle?"

I picked up our coffee cups and went to the kitchen. What could I say about Davy Hoyle? I'd read everything of his I could find and loved it. Even some of the loose ends and forgotten fables published after his death were in my study. I held him in awe. He was the finest writer I'd ever read. He could do things with the English language that were unbelievable.

Poe could create startlingly clear pictures with very few words. Hoyle was better. Unlike Poe, Hoyle's pictures were less startling, more beautiful. Instead of pictures, they were more like vast panoramas of beauty, fragrance, and sound. You could not only see what Hoyle wrote about; you could feel it.

We spent the next hour and a half talking of Hoyle - the beauty of his landscapes, the lure of his desert scenes, the strength and depth of his characters. We spoke of his plots, quick rise of action, and plummeting endings, of all we loved in his work.

She was a kindred spirit and an open, friendly air had tentatively developed between us. I was keeping some reservation in the back of my mind. This wasn't just two friends discussing a mutual interest. She was a stranger who wanted something. Yet, there was a thread of desire in me to continue. I hadn't shared such an intoxicating conversation in years. And this had lasted only...six hours!

I blinked and rechecked my watch. "Diana, you must be starved; it's eight o'clock."

"Oh, my!" she exclaimed. "I've got to make quite a few calls and take care of some other business. I must go!"

It was almost like it was midnight and the limo would turn into a pumpkin. She made a quick phone call and prepared to leave. I offered a dinner date but she refused.

Her impatience was somewhat unnerving. I hoped it wasn't her father driving the limo. She really seemed like a kid out past curfew.

She said she'd return at two the next afternoon and hurried out of the house as the limo approached.

Character Assassination

Chapter 3

It is loneliness that makes the loudest noise

~Eric Hoffer

I was very moody and a little sad. The few hours of good conversation about literature had been like a desert sunset. It was pleasant, beautiful, magnificent, and exhilarating but over much too quickly. Diana's sudden departure and cool, aloof attitude, like the cool desert night that followed one of those glorious sunsets, had left things chilled and dank.

I was coffee logged and tired. I wanted a drink but Scotch didn't seem to be what I wanted. I also decided I was hungry.

Half an hour later, I walked into a twenty-four-hour restaurant that served breakfast even at ten o'clock at night. This was my favorite kind of place. I took a booth in a dimly lit corner and ordered some eggs.

While I waited for the food, I got out my tablet. I always carried a pad in case I got an inspiration. I wasn't getting one then, but I thought the pad might help me focus.

The tablet was still blank when my eggs came. As I ate, I thought bitterly about the blank page. In the last two years, I'd had more blank pages than I cared to remember. Or worse yet, I'd had pages filled with poor writing. Jack London wrote fifty novels in fifteen years. I was awed at his pace and the energy he must have expended. A book a year is a lot of work. Most of his work had been good; a couple of books were really great - timeless classics. I couldn't match his record, but I knew I must continually produce. Since my divorce, I'd sold two books - both mysteries. They were mediocre at best but Chucky had gotten them published on my reputation. He had just closed a deal on the third one. It was no better than the first two, but Chucky had gotten a publisher in Wisconsin to handle it.

My career had started ten years ago just after I left the Army. I sold some small things - magazine articles and a couple of poems. Then I finished my first novel - a Western. I was a little surprised that it sold so quickly. It was good, very good, but I'd always heard how hard it was to break into the business. That book had taken two years to write. Shortly after it was published, I finished another Western. That's when I latched onto Chucky, or maybe he latched onto me. I'd sold my first novel by myself but hired an agent for the next one. My agent, a woman named Gayle Pike, had died shortly after selling the book. Somehow Chucky had picked up the pieces of Gayle's business. I'm sure he only took the lucrative pieces, but that included me.

Chucky sold my third novel and some miscellaneous things I'd written just after that I got married.

Harriet and I had known each other since college. We'd had sort of a hot-and-cold romance for about five years. Then we had a hot-and-cold marriage for another five years - mostly cold. When we divorced, I seemed to lose my creativity for about seven or eight months. I tried, but nothing with a Western theme suited me. When the Westerns weren't flowing, I had become Tip Thinn and wrote current-day mysteries. I forced a continuous march of words from my pen. In the last year and a half, I've written the three mysteries. They were alright, I guess, but certainly not my best work.

What had Diana said - I've been in a slump since the divorce. The truth is I haven't written anything worthwhile in months.

It was just last week that I had come upon a good idea and since then I've done some of my best writing. I think I had finally found my rhythm or something. Then Diana showed up and screwed up the flow. I shoved the half-eaten breakfast aside, picked up my blank tablet and left the diner.

I made up my mind not to accept Diana's offer, no matter what it was. She knew a lot about writing and about literature, but I couldn't imagine that she really had anything of any value to offer. I was getting back into a comfortable routine, I couldn't let her mess it up.

The Scotch at my favorite bar was good; the atmosphere was quiet. After a couple of drinks with a morose bartender, I felt better. By the time I got to the house, I was ready to write. It was a little after midnight and my creative juices were flowing. The new Western mystery in my word processor unfolded before me. Everything worked. I was back in the flow of writing.

I felt great!

It was morning when I stopped. I quit because I was writing about a place in southwest Colorado and I needed to do some research on the area. I was surprised when I noticed that it was eleven o'clock in the morning. I'd lost all track of time and of everything else.

Knowing the time really took the wind out of my sails. I was tired but when I realized how long I'd worked, the exhaustion caved in on me. As is so often the case, adrenaline comes on quickly and balloons you up. Then when some little thing comes along and seems to tear the inflated fabric, the power drains away even more quickly than it came.

I made a few notes for research and decided I'd better get ready. Diana would be here at two. Hopefully, she wouldn't take much of my time. I needed sleep badly. Surprisingly, I was no longer bitter about her invasion, nor was I enticed by our mutual interests. She was just an issue to be dealt with and eliminated.

Chapter 4

A word is not crystal, transparent, or unchanged; it is the skin of a living thought.

~Oliver Wendell Holmes

The "issue" again arrived promptly on time. She was wearing a gray business suit this time, but that was about the only change.

"Good afternoon, Mr. Noble." She stopped rather abruptly, then went on in a softer tone, "You look very tired. Are you feeling well?" There was a genuine concern in her voice.

"I'm fine. I worked all night and I'm very tired."

"What are you working on, John?"

"I'm doing a Western mystery. I'm afraid I spent all night on it and ..."

She cut me off gracefully. "Back to what you do best. I'm glad; may I read what you've done so far?"

"No! No one reads my work until it's finished." I expected one of her sharp retorts but it was strangely lacking. Instead, there seemed a softness in her eyes - an understanding of the protective nature all writers seemed to have for their work. I'd spoken a little more sharply than I had intended. I eased up and continued, "I'm doing very well with the new book and so I'm afraid I won't be able to take your offer."

The sharpness came flashing back in her voice and in her eyes. "You don't even know what my offer is, Mr. Noble, so you don't know that you don't want it."

"I know that I'm very busy, Mrs. Faire. I couldn't devote the time to your project and my own work. Therefore, whatever you're selling, I'm not buying."

"You turn down a million readers very easily." She paused and again caught me as I was ready to speak. "Mr. Noble, you're too tired to discuss the fate of so many loyal readers. I'll be back tomorrow at two."

I started to object but she waved off my argument and said, "If you'll give me one hour tomorrow, I'll present my case and accept your answer without question."

I reluctantly agreed and she asked to use the phone. As she waited for the limo, she said that I might have time for my work *and* her project if I combined them. I started to ask her to clarify that comment but the limo had just arrived.

After she'd gone, I wondered again about her departure. As soon as she had decided to go, she seemed nervous, almost like a jealous lover awaited and she had stayed too long.

It didn't bother me long, though. I was asleep at three o'clock.

Chapter 5

We must not inquire too curiously into motives ... they are apt to become feeble in the utterance.

~George Eliot

I woke up at midnight, spent a very creative, very productive eight hours and took a nap.

After a shower, breakfast and an hour of sorting mail into "pay these", "answer these", and "reread these" stacks, I stretched out on the sofa to relax. Two o'clock was still an hour away and I had decided to give Diana a fair hearing before I declined her offer. Although I fully intended to turn her down, I had to admit that she tickled my greed when she mentioned a million readers. She sure knew how to push the right buttons. I was also puzzled about her comment to combine the projects.

What did I know about her? She was young, probably not more than twenty-two or -three. Youth spoke of inexperience but she knew literature and was well schooled in the use of power. She was also very controlling or tried to be. The controlling attitude made me think she was spoiled and probably by wealthy parents.

Her outward appearance didn't give the impression of wealth. Her clothes were new and fit well but they were obviously department store stuff. She wore no jewelry - not even earrings or a wedding band, although she had said she was married. Her fingernails were real and I was sure she fixed them herself. Her hair was cut in a very simple, conservative style with nothing to indicate expensive salon treatments. The only things she showed that said money were the limo and the briefcase. The limo was probably rented, but still spoke of wealth, sort of.

She had never opened the briefcase. Whenever she came in, she sat it down on the floor. She never seemed to forget that it was there, but didn't seem to be guarding it either. The briefcase wasn't new but must have been gently handled and well cared for.

So what did I know about Mrs. Diana Faire? Not much really. She was attractive, maybe even pretty if she smiled. Her appearance made me think of the businesswoman, but her actions didn't support that idea completely. She had seemed from the first to want to march in, make a deal and leave. Yet, she hadn't ranted and raved about losing a day of work. As a matter of fact, it had been her idea. She had also lost track of time when we started talking about writing. Her sudden nervousness and rush to leave could be deadline oriented but I didn't think so. It just didn't feel that way.

Maybe the inconsistencies came from youth and inexperience. She might grow into the powerhouse business person she was trying to be. Yet, she had worked on Chucky successfully. As mad as I still was at him, I had to admit he was pretty shrewd about people and loyal to his clients. He was probably more loyal to the fees he charged his clients, but it came down to the same thing.

I started to get up and call him but I decided it would just aggravate me. I still wanted to give Mrs. Faire an honest listening to. Then I'd turn her down and call Chucky!

I stretched and reviewed the facts in *The Strange Case of Mrs. Diana Faire*. I still *knew* nothing. I had some hunches, but I knew nothing!

I hate mysteries.

I write mystery novels. Even my Westerns were just mystery stories set in the old West. But that was different. They weren't mysteries to me. I knew all of the secrets and if I didn't, I'd make some up. Committing the perfect crime is so simple - on paper. It could be easy in life also, but one would have to take care with the details. It's even more so when you control all the variables.

But even for all the annoyance of this mystery, I was glad to have one I couldn't see through. It's a humbling experience; good writers need that once in a while. At any rate, it was almost two o'clock and my involvement in this tale ended at three.

At three o'clock there would be one less person in my life and that was how I wanted it. People, even well-intentioned people, just complicate life!

Chapter 6

Compromise used to mean that half a loaf was better than no bread. Among modern statesmen, it really seems to mean that half a loaf is better than a whole loaf.

~*G. K. Chesterton*

Again she was prompt. She wore a light blue business suit. I noticed for the first time that all of her suits were identical except for the color. I watched her closely as she entered and went to the dining room table. I was trying to catch all of the clues I could. I knew I was just playing detective and the mystery would soon end, but I rationalized that I was researching the way some future character would think and act.

"You look much more rested, Mr. Noble."

"I feel better today, Mrs. Faire. Thank you for asking. Care for a coffee?"

"Please." Her tone was very businesslike; her actions very professional. There was a hardness in her features that indicated this was to be a strictly-business meeting.

When she picked up her cup, I saw a slight tremble. She was a little nervous. I again studied for clues and saw a strong-willed business person and credited the nervousness to being ready to close a very big deal - or lose it. I also noted that the briefcase was on the table.

She showed no signs of the jitters as she started laying the deal before me. "Mr. Noble, you're a very good writer. My father and I discussed your talent at length. We were always reviewing new literature; it was a hobby we had. At the time, I had no idea I would need your services." She faltered slightly and her features darkened momentarily.

When she had recovered her composure she continued in the same strong manner as before. I was sure she had rehearsed this sales pitch many times.

"When I arrived in San Antonio, I was convinced you were the writer I needed. My father thought highly of your talent. Mr. Stonemason agreed on the merit of the project and after our discussion, yours and mine, two days ago, I knew I'd found the answer to my dilemma." She stood and paced the floor.

I sat quietly and listened. I watched her pace and saw the excitement in her rise. She was thinking visibly as she paced. I could almost see her counting off the high points of the deal in her mind.

Her excitement was infectious. I was torn between emotions. On the one hand, she seemed so excited at how well things were going to work out in her dilemma and I almost felt compelled to help her. On the other hand, I hadn't heard anything convincing except a few compliments. Her father thought highly of me, but who was he? Chucky thought there was merit in the proposition which means there was money in it. I was still frustrated with good old Chucky, so his opinion carried less weight than usual. Yet Chucky had risked my anger, and maybe my business, to set up this meeting! There was something to this deal, I was sure!

Even after I heard the facts of the deal I would need some time to sort things out for myself. It was then I realized that I didn't have much time. Diana Faire had boxed me in. She said at the end of her hour she would accept my answer. So I was sort of forced to answer by that time.

I gave myself heck for being trapped again.

She abruptly stopped pacing and leaned on the table. "Mr. Noble, what I have to offer," she said as she stared unflinchingly into my eyes, "is eight well established Western characters. You'll know the names, and I own the copyrights outright. You'll have complete autonomy on plot, setting and character usage, as long as you don't violate their established biographies." She patted the briefcase and sat down.

I'd been offered some strange deals but this was the strangest one yet. What would I want with someone else's characters? I had a good sense of character development. How could somebody else's characters become mine? Would the readers stay loyal to characters instead of the author? Why would the author give them up if they carried so much promise? How had she obtained the copyrights? I'd never heard of a fictional character's biography being copyrighted.

This was just too much to absorb all at once. It sounded absurd on the surface but those are the kind of things that usually had a way of working out pretty well.

I took a deep breath and tried to organize my thoughts. I noticed that Diana was patiently watching me. It was as if she could see me struggling to get my thinking in order. I felt strangely naked before her penetrating gaze. Damn!

Another deep breath and a sip of coffee made me realize my hands were shaking, and that angered me. She had noticed too and that made me even madder. I gulped more coffee and she asked, "Any questions, John?"

"Quite a few. First, you said I'd recognize some names. Try me." If the names were unfamiliar, or I pretended they were, I'd feel more composed. I made up my mind to be ignorant.

"Karl Schwartz, John Pascoe, Wilson David and his brother Mason, Able Tucker, Kevin Cain, Homer Dent, and

Bedford. Any of those sound familiar?" She had spoken the names like a litany of past lovers, but the question was a challenge.

My composure was shot. Those were the famous eight of Davy Hoyle. At first, I was in a state of confused shock. The thought of having these characters for my own exclusive use was exciting and absurd all at once. But it quickly became more absurd than anything else, and I got angry for having wasted my time with this obviously demented woman. Then I got really mad for being treated like a fool.

How could Diana Faire have the copyrights to Hoyle's characters? Hoyle died two years ago in a car wreck, or a plane crash, or something like that. Hoyle had built sixty novels on those eight people. They weren't just characters; they were almost real people. They were the most famous fictional heroes in the Western literary world. But Hoyle had never sold any of his copyrights. Every book he'd written in the last twenty-five years of his life was about one or more of these eight. Hoyle would never have sold his bread-and-butter creations.

Damn her! This was a scam! It was a sadistic hoax of some kind for some unknown purpose, but I was through being played for the sucker! "I don't know what kind of charade you're involved in, but it's over as of now! Please leave!" I stood up and was too mad for even common courtesy.

She started to say something but I cut her off. "This meeting is over! I refuse your offer! Get out!"

She stood meekly and pulled her briefcase in front of her. "Before I go, please look at one document." She opened the briefcase and took out a green five- by seven-inch document with an official-looking seal on it.

"That little paper can't refute what I already know. I've been played for a sucker. You don't have the rights to Hoyle's copyrights; he never sold them. Get out or I'll call the police."

I didn't want the little trickster in my home or in my life for another moment. I reached over and pushed her briefcase closed. "Now!"

She latched the briefcase and turned toward the door. She had left her document on the table. I snatched it up and started after her. She must have heard me pick it up because she said over her shoulder, "One second to look at that paper or a lifetime of regret. The choice is yours, John."

Ray Alan Collins

Chapter 7

My conviction is this, people must go on or go under

~David Lloyd George

I faltered; curiosity won a momentary battle.

What I held was a birth certificate from the State of Indiana. I caught my breath as I read. The child's name was Diana Sue Hoyle; the father was listed as David C. Hoyle of Arizona.

Diana had kept walking toward the door, but if this was accurate, she was Davy Hoyle's child and probably heir to his copyrights.

"Wait!" I almost yelled the word. She stopped but didn't turn around. "Is this true?" I asked. "Are you Davy Hoyle's daughter?"

Still not turning, she asked, "Do you want to discuss business or heraldry?"

I realized she was fighting to control her emotions. She hadn't turned to face me for fear her face would give her away. She was winning a battle that was of supreme importance to her and the nearness of victory was unnerving. I proceeded carefully. "I think they are too intertwined to discuss separately. Please, come and sit down."

During the next three hours, we discussed the business aspects of building on a known character base. I hadn't decided this wasn't a scam, but I was sure I couldn't leave it alone until I knew. If it was a hoax, and I was afraid it was, I would feel like killing Diana.

She told me her mother was Hoyle's second wife. He had two daughters from his first wife, but she, Diana, had ended up with all of his copyrights. There was a coldness in her eyes and in her tone when she talked about her half-sisters. All she would say was that they each got enough of Hoyle's business interests to be filthy rich. I asked a couple of questions about them and their mother, but Diana wouldn't say anything.

"They never cared about Daddy's work or anything he did. As long as they had money, they didn't think of anyone else." Again that frosty tone so I didn't ask any more.

I had to call Chucky and he may know more about this. Thinking about Chucky brought me back to the present. I had a lot to do. She had already told me how she wanted to split the royalties and a number of other points in the deal. I didn't much like them, but we could negotiate.

"Diana, it's getting late and I've got a lot of work to do. I'm very interested in your deal, but I'll have to think about it."

She smiled that businesswoman smile and said, "You mean you've got to check me out." It wasn't a question or an accusation just a business fact.

"Yes, and of course I've got to talk to my lawyer. I've also got to pick up my kids for the weekend."

"I was hoping to work this weekend ..."

"Sorry. I've got daddy duty and that comes first."

"I understand," she said and I believed her. She drew a folder out of her briefcase and laid it on the table. "I had my lawyers draw up a contract. All you need to do is look it over and sign it."

"I thought Chucky told you I was a good businessman," I smiled at her. "I'll look this over, but I don't like some of the terms you've already mentioned. I'll have a counter proposal ready on Monday or Tuesday if everything checks out and I decide to accept."

She started to protest but I was waiting for her and started first. "It's getting late and I've got a lot to do. Give me a call Monday afternoon."

She didn't argue but seemed to realize that it was past six o'clock. Again she got impatient to leave. She paced and was pensive until the limo arrived. Then, she hurried out the door and was gone.

* * *

I rang Harriet's doorbell at nine o'clock. She let me in and I could tell she was mad about something. The twins came running in and hugged me.

"We didn't think you were coming, Daddy," squealed Amanda.

"Why would you think that, darling? Daddy's right on time." I realized that whatever had worried them had something to do with Harriet being angry. Before they could answer, I told them to go get their things.

As soon as they were gone, Harriet started grilling me about the "blond in the fancy car" who had spent the week at my house. The only way Harriet could have known about Diana was from Vivian. Vivian was my next-door neighbor. The whole time I had been married to Harriet, she and Vivian had been back-fence gossips. Vivian was a busybody and I doubted if a bird could fly through our neighborhood without her knowing about it. But knowing wasn't enough for her - she had to tell it, too. Harriet wanted to know all the dirt on everyone but she was too lazy to dig it up herself. The two of them became fast friends because they complimented each other so well. The only change in their relationship since Harriet moved away was that they did business over the phone instead of over the back fence. Vivian blamed me for the divorce - probably more than Harriet blamed me!

When Harriet had sort of gotten her anger off her chest, I said, "Give my regards to Vivian. And while you're at it, tell her we're not married any longer. As for the blond in the fancy car," I continued after a dramatic pause, "that's none of your business!"

"Forgive me, John," she sighed. It's been a tough week. Amanda's had a fever. Oh, just everything. I'm sorry." She still had that quick temper, but she seemed to cool off pretty fast for a change. Maybe she was changing.

The twins came back bursting with energy and ready to go. We got some hamburgers and a couple of videos before going back to the house.

A half hour after we started watching the movies both of them were sound asleep. They had their own schedule and I adjusted to it on the weekends that I had them.

Chapter 8

There is nothing like staying at home for real comfort

~ *Jane Austen*

At eight o'clock the next morning, I was up and cooking everybody's favorite breakfast - whatever that favorite happened to be at the time - when the phone rang. I figured it was Harriet. She always came up with some contrived emergency when I had the kids. It ranged from things like who she should get to do her taxes next year to who was the guy who played Hoss on *Bonanza*. Each time she called she talked to each of the kids briefly. I was sure she questioned them about my activities but they never mentioned it, nor did I. They had enough heartache in their lives without being a push-me-pull-you for their parents.

This had been a week for surprises. The phone call was the next one. The voice on the other end of the phone said, "John, this is Chucky. How are you?"

I recovered from the surprise quickly and remembered the kids were within earshot of me. I also noted he called himself "Chucky." Even though he allowed his best clients to call him that, I'd never heard him use the nickname himself. He knew I was mad and wanted to bury the hatchet.

"Mr. Stonemason, I've been trying to contact you since Wednesday. Since you haven't returned my calls, I assume you're no longer interested in my business. I'll have my attorney draw up the paperwork to immediately dissolve our dealings. Good day." I hung up the phone before he could bluster and explain. I also turned on the answering machine.

I had no intention of cutting him loose. He was the best agent around. However, I figured a little grief would do him some good.

I couldn't let him squirm too long because he would certainly know some things about Diana that I wanted to know. He was also in the best position to advise me on what this deal really consisted of. I would fax him a copy of the proposal and counter proposal after I let him off the hook - and after I talked to my lawyers.

I had already faxed the proposal to my lawyers. They would take the weekend to go over Diana's version of the deal. I told them the percentages I wanted and the concessions I expected. After that, I left it in their hands. They were my agents in legal matters - I told them what I wanted and they decided how to write the counter-proposal with enough padding to dicker. By Monday morning they would have everything ready so I spent the rest of the weekend playing daddy.

There was a Fourth of July fireworks extravaganza at Sea World. I had tickets and spent all of Saturday afternoon and evening at the water park with the twins.

By Sunday evening, I was sick of video games and junk food. We had spent the afternoon at the zoo, gone to the movies, ate pizza and I don't know what else. It seemed like no matter what else we did, we always ended up playing video games. I loved spending time with the twins but the games made me crazy. I played pinball and pool, even card games, but these electronic games were beyond my skills. Even when I just watched, the kids drew me into the web of the game. They would squeal, "Oh, Daddy, look at where I got to." or "Look at this ..." It all looked like the same confused pattern of little men moving, jumping, and running, or doing something else equally erratic. But the kids loved the games and I loved the kids, so I tolerated the insanity.

The weekend went quickly. As I pulled into Harriet's driveway, I was surprised that she hadn't called me all weekend. For that matter, neither had Diana or Chucky.

The kids went quietly back into their world of boredom after giving me a hug. Harriet was agreeable - almost patronizing. Oh, she asked a few questions but not the typical accusing, irritating kind she was so wont to ask. I spent a few minutes talking to her before I left.

Even though it hadn't been the usual kind of chat, I felt relieved to be out of her house - and out of her presence. She had always been overbearing and she made me feel uncomfortable. But, I thought, I still don't usually feel the strain until I leave. While I'm there, I'm keyed up and ready for an attack or treachery of some description. When I leave and relax is when I realize how much of a strain being near her causes me.

I wondered if Diana felt the same way about me. If so, that could explain why she always felt so rushed to leave. I pondered on that idea as I drove back home. Diana was still a mystery to me.

The answering machine had just started taking a call as I walked in. It was Chucky pleading for me to answer. I did and found out he was in town to see me. He said he knew I kept crazy hours and wanted to come to see me right away.

He was here because of Diana; he didn't say so but it figured. It also figured that if Chucky had come out here on a weekend, there was money in the deal - a lot of money. I gave him directions and told him I needed an hour to put away my groceries.

After my household chores, I checked the messages on my machine. There were twelve of them - seven from Chucky. It seemed like most of the people who hadn't called me over the weekend made up for it in the last few hours.

Vivian had called and said she thought she saw someone in my backyard. Harriet had called and wanted to know what time I was bringing the twins home. There was a call from Diana. She said her lawyers would be in town Monday and Tuesday. She wanted a business supper Monday evening and had made the reservations.

Leo Donaldson, my business manager, called to let me know the electrical work being done on my self-storage warehouse had been postponed. Leo had great business sense. I trusted him completely, and he handled all my business interests that didn't involve writing. He knew I trusted his judgment but he always called to fill me in on the little, day-to-day details.

The last call was from my lawyers. They wanted to know my feelings on the death clause in the contract Diana had given me. I had no feelings on the matter because I hadn't read it closely enough to see any kind of a death clause.

I got out my copy of the contract and was studying it when Chucky showed up. He brought a gift - a bottle of my brand of Scotch. I wasn't sure if his mother had taught him well, or if it was a peace offering. That didn't matter; he might be able to shed some light on my mystery.

Maybe even on a mutual death clause.

Chapter 9

What has happened once will invariably happen again.

~*Abraham Lincoln*

We talked most of the night. Chucky was excited about the contract and about the deal in general.

When I asked about the death clause, he thought for a while before he answered. He told me he couldn't say for sure, but he knew there was bad blood between Diana and her half-sisters.

"The older sisters, from Hoyle's first marriage, hated the old man because he remarried immediately after their mother's death. His new wife was around thirty and he was probably fifty. From what I hear, the young wife was a heavy spender and the girls figured her for a gold-digging so-and-so." Chucky sipped his drink.

"By the time Hoyle and his new wife had been married for five years, the older girls were both married and Diana was about three. Those two girls, the older ones, were rich - Hoyle spoiled them and they never wanted for anything. They were pretty mean to Diana and her mother. Hoyle just wanted peace in his family so he packed up and moved to Indiana. He and his wife had been researching a story there when Diana was born. He liked this little burg called Bluffton, and when he left Arizona, that's where he went.

"Distance didn't solve the problem and over the next seventeen years, the family feud continued. It started getting to Hoyle and he escaped into his writing and into a bottle. There was some talk that he was drunk when he and his wife died. I don't know if that's true or not but it seems the older daughters believed it and blamed Diana.

"I believe that was just more meanness on their part. However, when the old man's Last Will and Testament was read and Diana inherited the copyrights, the sisters contested the will. They probably just wanted her left out, but she outfoxed them. She beat them in court and outside the courthouse got into a fist fight with them. Whipped both of them before their bodyguards could stop it. At least, that's the way I heard it." Chucky smiled. He admired spunk in others, especially women.

"Bodyguards?" I asked. "Were they in such constant peril?"

Chucky could tell I was both skeptical and amused. The excesses that people go to have always struck me with humor.

"This family fight has gone on for quite a while and the battles have taken place everywhere. None of them are overly civilized on family matters." There was a short pause before Chucky said, "None of them!"

After a long pause to let the warning settle itself in my mind, he went on, "There's every reason to believe she'd rather have you, as her partner, inherit the copyrights than for her family to get anything. I'm only guessing but that's the best I can do."

He seemed to have more to tell about Diana's life, and I wanted to know, but Chucky was here on business and that's where the conversation went for the next little while.

We discussed my counter proposal and Chucky approved. "I put out some feelers before I came out here and by the time I get back we should have some interesting propositions."

I showed my disgust. Chucky knew I hated to meet deadlines and if he got me some kind of an advance deal, that's what

I'd be stuck with. "Chucky, I haven't struck a deal with Diana, yet."

"You will, John. You will. Besides what do you do first? Have the baby or build the nursery?"

When Chucky started his back-woods analogies, it was time to see him to the door. As the Yellow Cab pulled away from the curb and whisked Chucky into a starlit south Texas night, I felt some better. I liked Chucky in spite of his obsession with big money and big deals. Yet even with him, I got that restless yearning to be alone - without any people in my life. He was one of the few friends I had, but despite our mutual liking of each other, it was a friendship of convenience. I needed him to advance my career; he needed to advance my career to meet his own personal and business goals.

I was glad he was gone so I could be alone, yet I was very glad he had come. He had filled in some of the gaps in the mystery surrounding Diana. I wasn't sure I liked her death clause, but as long as my lawyers wrote it to protect everything else of mine, I could live with the clause. Moreover, if Chucky was right, as extreme as his story sounded, and she wanted to be sure her sisters couldn't kill her for the copyrights, that meant I had a powerful bargaining chip.

I made a quick note to call Sam Twilly, the head of my legal staff, and then looked over Saturday's mail. After that, I wandered around the house doing odd chores that always seemed to accumulate when I was working.

I thought about that. Diana had brought turmoil into my life, but my work level was way up since I'd met her. Not only was I working harder, but I was also writing what I loved and doing it very well. Maybe I needed the kind of stress that pushy women cause.

I compared Diana and Harriet. Harriet is pushy, manipulative, and very self-centered. She always wanted to control everyone and everything around her. Before and during the divorce, I was seeing a psychologist who told me that Harriet's lifestyle was a textbook case of the adult-child of an alcoholic. Harriet's parents were both alcoholics so she is really an emotional mess. Diana, on the other hand, wasn't really pushy and manipulative. She had learned those ways as business tools and could employ them with some success. But they weren't natural for her and they didn't have the same sting Harriet gave them. As much as I hated Harriet, she had given me a kind of drive I haven't had since the divorce.

Until Diana …

* * *

I slept a little later than usual and had about three hours to get ready for Diana's business supper. Before laying down, I had called Twilly and told him about the supper and the way I wanted to handle the death clause. Actually, I told his answering machine but I knew he would make the meeting. He was the sort of guy who would go to extremes to do a good job for his clients. He seemed to know a little about all areas of law and usually had answers to questions before the clients formulated the questions. Finding him had been a real stroke of luck for me.

I checked my machine and found a scattering of pretty routine messages. Diana had called to confirm the meeting this evening. I realized she had never told me where she was staying or given me a phone number. I hoped she would call back so I could tell her that Chucky and Sam Twilly would be there. Of course, she probably figured I'd have a large entourage.

Chapter 10

We have met the enemy and he is us.

~*Walt Kelly*

Chucky was waiting for the elevator when I entered the Tower of the Americas. He looked like he always did - dressed and ready for business. We were the only two in the private elevator that took diners up to the exclusive restaurant atop the tower. When we got out of the elevator, Sam was in the lobby of the restaurant.

Sam told me he was just glad he could accept my invitation. He spoke like I'd invited him to my home for a barbecue. But that was the way he always was. He liked me and liked doing business with me. Unlike Chucky, however, Sam didn't give the impression that business and money were always in his thoughts. I suspected Sam liked most people and enjoyed himself as well.

"Sam, this is my agent, Charles Stonemason. Chucky, Sam Twilly, my attorney." They shook hands and we started into the restaurant.

Sam was wearing a forest-green, double-breasted suit with a tie of the same color. There was an emerald tie tack about an inch below the knot, and he wore a white shirt.

Sam was two inches taller than my six feet, while Chucky was that much shorter. I was a lean one hundred sixty, while both my companions were heavy. I had discarded my jeans and boots for my most fashionable suit. I knew we made an impressive sight, and anywhere else in town folks would have taken notice. But here, in this fancy rotating restaurant at the top of the Tower, we were commonplace in both dress and demeanor.

The maître d' showed us to the table where Diana and her group were sitting. I had to hand it to her, she was sitting in the power chair.

She was wearing an off-the-shoulder, white gown. There was a string of pearls at her throat, and with all the white linen, cut glass, and silver on the table, she looked like she'd been built first and all the trappings added to suit her. It was just an impression, but a very effective impression of power and position. Damn, she was good; this was surely no accident.

There were four men sitting with her and all were dressed to fit the occasion and place. I started the introductions as soon as we were seated. She knew Chucky, of course, but I introduced him for the benefit of the others.

I could see Diana didn't like the idea of Chucky being here. She must have thought I'd hauled in a ringer for the meeting. There wasn't much in her behavior to indicate her irritation, but I noted a fleeting something in her eyes that told me she didn't like it. Whatever it was, it seemed to have disappeared as quickly as it appeared.

She smiled sweetly and said, "Charles, it's wonderful to see you again, although I'm surprised you came all the way to Texas for such a routine meeting." I could see that high-powered business wasn't all she had been schooled in. She was charming and that seemed alright with Chucky.

"You're looking lovely as usual, Mrs. Faire." Chucky sounded oily and ready to propose to her. "But, I'm here on vacation. John has always bragged about Texas and this lovely city. I decided to see it for myself. I must admit he wasn't just a bragging Texan; my wife and I are having a wonderful time. When John told me of this meeting, well, I couldn't pass up the chance to see you again." He finished with sort of an embarrassed air. I was also beginning to think I was the only one at the table who wasn't a con artist.

I introduced Sam Twilly and added, "Diana, you might be interested to know Mr. Twilly is also from Indiana." Even though he had been living in Texas since graduating from law school twenty-five years ago, I wanted to inject some new conversational items into this meeting.

"I'm very pleased to meet you Mr. Twilly. My father was a big college football fan and had heard of you." Then, to me, she said, "College football is a big deal in Arizona, John. My father loved it and took the passion with him when he moved to Indiana."

Sam added, for my benefit, "In Indiana, everyone gets excited about high school basketball." Then to Diana, he said, "I'm surprised anyone at all remembers me as a football player, Mrs. Faire. I'm flattered."

"Daddy liked football, and frankly, he studied athletes quite a bit, kept notes, that sort of thing. He studied people to build characters for his books. Most of the people he wrote about were made up from the best parts of several people. If I remember correctly, Mr. Twilly, you played guard for two years before your back injury."

"Your father kept good notes, Mrs. Faire. I got hurt in the first game of my junior year. The injury was only minor, but I realized I didn't want to be a big-league ballplayer. I had a bigger love for the law than football. Everything between then and now has been pretty commonplace, but I'm happy." He paused then asked, "Did Mr. Hoyle build somebody out of me?"

There was polite laughter before Diana replied, "If he didn't, Mr. Twilly, he should have."

I knew Sam hadn't played college ball in thirty years and Hoyle only moved to Indiana about twenty years ago. Hoyle may have studied all college athletes, but I was pretty sure Diana's story was made up. But it did show she had done her homework for this meeting.

Diana introduced her legal staff. The first two were lawyers from Indianapolis, the third an Arizona attorney that I guessed she had inherited from Hoyle along with the copyrights. I found out later from Sam that I'd guessed right. The fellow was a well-known patent and copyright attorney.

The last man she introduced was a surprise. I'd heard of Anthony Milford for years but had never seen him. He was a prominent business lawyer here in San Antonio. His firm represented some of the largest business interests in south Texas.

With the introductions done and the drinks ordered, Diana started the preliminaries. These sorts of meals always amazed me. Everyone who ran one seemed to think they had come up with an original agenda. Unfortunately, they always had the same pattern and only the faces changed.

We were going to chit-chat through dinner and discuss business over some after-dinner drinks. Knowing this was a help because I could take over the situation whenever I chose to - if I chose to. I settled down to eat and engage in whatever chatter came my way. I was basically an introvert and had forced myself to learn the social necessities. Now that I knew them, I used them when they suited my purpose. I felt this evening was a time to be reserved and quiet.

Chucky was mingling well and keeping an eye on me at the same time. He wanted to be sure I used the right fork. Chucky handled about a half dozen of the best Western writers in the country, yet for all his success in our area of literature,

Chucky had never learned that we were not just old cowboys right in off of the range.

His convenient lie during the introductions, I finally realized, was for my benefit. Diana knew he was here on business - this business - but the way he was gushing over her was having its effect. I knew, from the fib he had told about his wife being here, that his moonstruck act was just that - an act. He had come up a notch in my opinion as I watched him manipulate the gathered crowd. I was also seeing why my career was so successful.

I decided to let the evening run the way Diana had planned it and trust Chucky and Sam to catch some flies with honey that I could only catch with vinegar, if at all. I had always been the bull in business. I just charged in and attacked. I'd almost always been successful and had never had to learn business finesse. The idea of trusting others when I was in the room was foreign to me. All in all, this was going to be an interesting evening.

When the after-dinner drinks were on the table, Diana asked, "John, have you considered my proposal?"

"Yes, Diana, I have and Mr. Twilly was so kind as to draft my counter-proposal. As I told you on Friday, there were certain aspects of your offer that I took exception to." Even though I'd vowed to let my agents handle the meeting, I couldn't pass up the vinegar altogether. "Sam, if you'll explain the changes we've made to Mrs. Faire's offer, I'll be back in a moment." Then to the group, I asked to be excused.

As I was stepping away from the table, I heard Sam say he had made copies of my offer and highlighted the changes from Diana's proposal. Count on Sam to be ready for anything. I went to the men's room and wasted a few minutes.

When I returned, the table had been cleared and everyone had a manila folder in front of them. Diana, Chucky and the two lawyers from Indiana had their folders open on the table and were turning the pages or reading a passage here or there. Bob Tuttle, the Arizona lawyer, was furiously scrawling little notes on his copy. Milford's copy was unopened on the table in front of him, and he and Sam were discussing San Antonio's new professional football franchise.

Chucky closed his folder and poured himself some coffee from the decanter on the table. After tasting the coffee, he leaned toward me and said in a husky whisper, "I think you've made a good offer, John."

Even though he had whispered, it was loud enough for all to hear. His comment was a crack in the dam. Little pockets of quiet conversation erupted all around the table. Chucky lowered his voice and started talking to me. I almost laughed because he was still leaning toward me and occasionally he would accent something he was saying by tapping on my manila folder. The funny part was that he was talking about seeing the Alamo before flying back to New York.

I was only half listening to Chucky but he was playing his part so it didn't matter. Bayless and Higginbotham, the fellows from Indiana, were in a whispered conversation that I couldn't hear at all. Tuttle was chatting a mile a minute at Diana and waving his hands in wild gestures. I could only pick up a word or two of what he was saying, but he seemed to approve of the deal. Milford was still discussing football with Sam.

Diana laughed at something Tuttle said. That caught me a little off guard; he just didn't seem like a very funny person. Higginbotham looked up when she laughed and they started a low conversation with Bayless looking on. Tuttle, like an obedient pet who had been ordered off the porch, went back to making little notes.

Diana's face showed that she wasn't enjoying what Higginbotham had to say nearly as much as Tuttle's witty remark. Bayless opened up his folder to the last page and pushed it toward her. Higginbotham tapped the page and explained something.

The death clause was on the last page and I had cut it out altogether. I'm sure that was what was causing the commotion at the other end of the table. Diana picked up the folder that had been pushed to her and read from the last page.

She seemed a little shaken as she closed the folder and placed it on the table in front of her. She took a couple of deep breaths and picked up a spoon. When she tapped her water glass, Sam and Milford broke off their conversation, Tuttle closed his folder and pocketed his pen, while Chucky and I turned our attention to our hostess.

"Gentlemen, shall we discuss business?" She paused while we all shifted in our chairs to physically as well as mentally change modes from conversation to business. "John, I'd like to go over your proposal point by point. We only need to discuss the items you've changed as I assume you're willing to accept the others as they are."

I agreed and we droned through most of the points. In each case, we agreed or haggled some, then agreed. I was impressed with the way she ran the meeting and kept everything on track.

In the first fourteen pages of the contract, the only long discussion we had was over my percentage of the royalties. I'd set my share high - very high. But with Chucky speaking as the expert and the lawyers doing some legal fencing, we agreed on a percentage acceptable to both of us. It was still high. In fact, it was higher than I expected to get or would have settled for.

Then the fifteenth and final page came up. The death clause was the only item left to discuss and I knew there was going to be a fight.

"John, I see you've deleted the death clause. That is unacceptable." Her voice had lost all of its charm and taken on an edge.

"I didn't like the clause and *it's* what I find unacceptable." I kept my voice calm and friendly. I'd practiced that line most of the evening.

Higginbotham interjected quickly, "Mr. Noble, there are certain, uh, personal conditions which caused Mrs. Faire to include that clause in the contract. We need not dredge up family matters, but it is in the best interests of my client. I insist on the clause."

Sam was the next one to speak. "Be that as it may, Mrs. Faire," he intentionally ignored Higginbotham, "my client has certain professional considerations that cause him to reject the death clause. He will lose considerable revenue over the next year to eighteen months to do the writing you wish done. If his untimely demise should be within that period the death clause would severely burden his estate."

The debate continued for another forty-five minutes without anyone gaining any ground. Neither Milford nor Tuttle really took part in the discussion. Tuttle struck me as a somewhat single-minded man. His area of expertise was copyrights and the contract seemed to suit him. The death clause was a business or family matter and therefore not in his bailiwick. He did, however, continue to scribble on his copy of the contract. I wanted to get up and walk around the table to see if he was still making notes or just doodling. I still couldn't figure out exactly why Milford was here. He didn't seem to be doing anything to earn his fee.

I finally got tired of the chatter. When I spoke, my voice was cold and hard. "Diana, we could beat this point endlessly. The fact is you want me to agree to something I don't want and you don't want to tell me why." Higginbotham started to interrupt and I'd had enough of him so I just raised my voice and continued. "I don't know what you're afraid of. I don't know if it's a persecution complex, a screwball family, or what, but I do know I'm not signing a contract with a death clause in it until I've got the full story. This meeting is over!" I stood up and headed for the bar with Sam and Chucky, reluctantly, in tow.

Before I'd taken my first step, Diana had leaped from her chair and started screaming. I must say, for a delicate young lady, she knew some violent language. People were staring from one to the other of us as I pulled out a barstool and ordered a drink.

Bayless was trying to get her calmed down but she was determined to follow me into the bar and have a cat fight. Higginbotham was just as mad as she was and it dawned on me that the old goat had a crush on her. Tuttle was bewildered and embarrassed. Milford sat at the table staring into his drink.

Diana had knocked over her chair when she jumped up. The maitre d' had righted it by the time she got into the barroom area. I smiled inwardly and wondered if a place this classy had a bouncer.

As she approached me, fists clenched, tears on her cheeks, and still screaming obscenities, Higginbotham was at her side. Bayless was like a herd dog trying to turn a two-sheep stampede without any luck.

I turned my stool around to face her and just let her rant. When she'd just about run out of steam, I spoke up. "Little girl, I don't know whether you've got a death wish or an Oedipus Complex, but you're the one who can explain it or forget it. Period!" I swung my barstool back around and tossed off my Scotch.

Diana was whimpering and being led away. Higginbotham hissed, "Bastard! I'll see you in court."

I told him he'd better get a good lawyer and ordered another drink.

Sam cast a sidelong glance at me and I could tell he thought I'd been too rough on Diana. And frankly, I had been more severe than I intended. As much as I wanted this deal for my ego's sake, it still looked like something that could slow down the work I was most interested in doing. Chucky had a worried look on his face and kept poking the ice in his drink with his index finger. I knew he was thinking in business terms and considered this deal lost. I didn't know if we had lost the contract and I was still confused over whether or not I wanted it, I just didn't know and I told myself I didn't care. I decided this was trial by combat. If I got the deal, I'd take it. If I didn't, I wouldn't lose any sleep over it.

It was getting late and I wanted to go home and write. I couldn't leave this bar, however, with the feelings of Chucky and Sam hanging. I respected their opinions and valued their friendship so I asked Sam, "Do you want to kick me first?" I expected him to make some half-hearted attempt to apologize for my action and then express his opinion.

I was wrong!

"Yes, John, I do." He swiveled his stool toward me and fixed me with a level gaze. "You were mean to that young lady. Cruel. I've known you for a long time, John Noble, and I've seen you bull your way through some tough deals, but you were just cruel to gain an advantage."

"You told me this morning you could live with that stupid death clause and that you intended to use it as a bargaining chip. Damn it, John, you got everything you wanted and more. There was no need to act like you did.

"I've rewritten the clause to your specifications and if it's added to the contract, you're fully protected. But, John, you owe Mrs. Faire an apology."

I looked over at Chucky. He didn't look up. He just kept poking his drink and said, "I agree."

"So do I." The voice came from behind me. I spun around to see Milford standing behind me with a drink in his hand. I got mad but he saw it and held up his hands in submission. "I'm not here to eavesdrop, Noble. In fact, I came to tell you that you're going to get the contract. Tuttle is the copyright guy and he likes it. Mrs. Faire likes the deal, but she feels she must be protected from her sisters. Bayless is mad at you but he likes the deal. Higginbotham hates you so his opinion doesn't count."

"And where do you stand, Milford?" I really wanted to know but asked more as a challenge. I didn't know how he fit into the team. He was a mystery and I hate mysteries.

"I'm not here for the deal, but if they ask, I like it." He didn't embellish his position and made it rather obvious that he didn't intend to.

"So you figure I've got the contract?" I asked.

He smiled, "They went back to their hotel and they'll kick it around for a few hours, but she needs you. If you add the clause back in, you've got the deal." He waved and walked away.

I couldn't figure where he fit in this whole thing which made me angry.

I hate mysteries!

Chapter 11

Let us never negotiate out of fear.

~John F. Kennedy

I've never been given to self-analysis. I'd always just done things the way that seemed best and never tried to figure out why. I always tried to remember what worked and with whom, but that was all. Things, especially in business, had always seemed to work my way. I learned years ago to trust my instincts and bull in.

By two the next afternoon I had slept well, showered, ate, and accomplished nothing. The way I had treated Diana bothered me. The fact that my friends had chastised me for it bothered me too, but not as much.

Most of my waking hours since I had left the restaurant had been consumed with trying to figure myself out. I'd never done business with a woman before; maybe I wasn't any harder on her than on the men I'd dealt with. If that was the case then I didn't want to do business with women.

Not even Diana?

No! I wanted to do business with her. I was sitting around hoping she would call so I could apologize.

Before leaving the bar, I told Sam to rewrite my counter offer to meet my original demands without the padding and include the death clause. He warned me she may be busy drafting another offer based on what was agreed on before the fight.

He also frowned upon me giving up the gains I'd made during the meeting. "You can't pay her off in lieu of the apology you owe; she won't accept charity for your insults."

He was right, but I didn't care. I was going to give her a fair deal - if she still wanted a deal at all. I had treated her badly; I had not lived up to the Cowboy ethic I had always strived for. Cutting off my own gains wasn't part of the ethic, either, but it was a starting point. Women in the old West were few and far between. They, like any scarce commodity, were treated gently as a rule. I had violated that rule!

I always cast myself in the role of the cowboy hero. Cowboys, real cowboys, not the Urban variety of today, were careful and respectful to the few women they encountered. There were, obviously, some hard cases who thought differently, but I wasn't one of those types. Was I?

I tried to appease my conscience by reminding myself that this was the 1990s, not the 1870s and nobody really knew I had violated my personal standards of behavior. It didn't work - I knew!

I was lost in this train of thought when I realized the phone was ringing. I hurried to answer it.

"John, this is Diana. May I come over; we've got to talk." She sounded meek but strangely excited.

"Diana, I want to talk - to apologize to you. I was brutal without a reason. I don't want to talk here, however. I'd like to meet you somewhere else: your hotel, a restaurant, anywhere. Please!"

We agreed to meet at a diner. She seemed to perk up a little when we'd finished talking. She was still pretty meek, but maybe some better.

I drove my Cadillac rather than the truck. I was giddy and awkward, but I knew I wouldn't have any peace until I'd set this right with Diana - and with myself. I called Sam from the car and ask him to stand by in case I needed him.

In the back corner of a greasy diner, I started our conversation with a long, sincere apology. For her part, she sat and listened without interruption. Her eyes stayed on my face and she seemed to grow almost excited. When I finished, our waiter came to the table and Diana asked me to order for both of us. I felt a little strange because I had no idea what she wanted or if she had likes or dislikes. I didn't know if she had ever eaten in a dumpy little place like this before. I honored her request and hoped for the best.

When the waiter had left, she smiled and took a deep breath. "John, I want to tell you about my family." When I started to interrupt she stopped me. "It's important. Important to me and to our business." I decided this was as necessary for her as my need to ask her forgiveness had been for me. I just sat there and listened.

"Before I start telling you my turbulent family history, I want you to know I accept your apology and you're forgiven. What you did is exactly the kind of personal attack my father would have used, and I've tried to do the same thing to you a couple of times but you're so thick skinned you just turned it aside. More than ever, I'm convinced you're the man I want to finish Daddy's work."

She got down to the family history then, and it was certainly turbulent. She talked for almost an hour, only pausing when the waiter brought our food or refilled our coffee cups. In that first hour, she didn't tell me anything I hadn't already heard from Chucky.

She excused herself as the waiter cleared the table and brought more coffee. I remember thinking as she walked back to the table how really lovely she looked. She wore a yellow flowered sundress and sandals. Her hair was loose, as always, and she moved with an ease and grace that was youthful and innocent. The restaurant was starting to get busy with the supper crowd and more than a couple of men stole covert glances at Diana's lovely figure.

She sipped her coffee and started back on her narrative right where she had left off. Right away I started hearing things I hadn't heard from Chucky - things I'm sure he didn't know.

She told me more about her short and one-sided marriage than I really wanted to know. I thought it was something of a diversion in her story because I had a feeling the last part, covering the time since her father's death was hard for her to put into words. I listened to the tale of ill-fated love and infidelity. She had married the guy as a rebellious gesture against her mother. Her doting father had approved, as he had approved all the things she had done.

I was getting a picture of a little girl who had shown interest in her father and his work at an early age. If Diana was correct, the first Mrs. Hoyle had been a socialite and didn't spend much time or interest in what Davy had done. Her daughters, Beth and Sarah, had followed in her path and somewhat ignored their father for the glamour of social life with their mother. The old man was probably very lonely and desperately looking for someone to share his interests.

By all accounts, his second wife was just such a person - and Diana even more so. At that point, he would probably have been a very contented old man except for the friction between his two families, and a growing problem between Diana and her mother. She didn't say anything specifically about the distant relationship she had with her mother. But it was obvious to me she was jealous of her parent's relationship. That jealousy was manifestly against her mother and I believed Diana had gone to great lengths to learn how to be the super-companion her father longed for.

Diana would have been shocked to hear that idea, though. I was pretty sure it was a subconscious drive. As I said, she never said anything pointedly against her mother - it was just a feeling I was developing.

Of course, all of this was just conjecture on my part. We often find a few facts or feelings and build a convenient theory on them only to find out we were wrong in the first place. Usually, we're wrong because we didn't have enough facts or because we, all of us, like known or accepted theories rather than new and unusual ones. I was going to make a point of rereading everything Hoyle had written in the last fifteen years. Often the things going on in a writer's life find their way into the characters and plots he develops. With Hoyle, I'd have to look for loneliness and a want of companionship in his old characters - the ones developed before he married Diana's mother. The family feuding and bitterness, if it showed up at all, would be in his newer characters. That would be a bit of a problem because the newer ones weren't his main characters and therefore weren't as fully developed.

We left the restaurant because we couldn't talk over the racket of the evening crowd at the diner. In the car, she called Bayless and told him to meet us at Sam's office. I called Sam and told him we'd struck an agreement and we were on our way over.

I commented on the fact that she had told Bayless to come alone. She told me Higginbotham was still very angry at me and might make a scene. "He's a wonderful old fellow and a very nice man, but he has a bad temper." It was obvious she thought of him as sort of a Dutch uncle.

"I don't know much about the law or about your Mr. Higginbotham," I told her. "But I know men, and that old man is in love with you."

"He adores me and since Daddy died he sees himself as my protector. Oh, sure, he's got a crush on me, but he doesn't expect anything from it. He's just a sweet old man with a fantasy and I allow him to keep it."

I didn't altogether agree but that was her business. I told her I was just glad he wasn't coming.

"Don't be too hard on him. I'll just keep you two apart." She had been talking happily but changed to a more serious tone and continued, "There's something else about my family you have to know, John."

"I told you before, Diana, you don't need to open up your personal life to me. I don't understand the forces that make you want a death clause in our contract, but I don't need to understand them. The way Sam has rewritten the clause protects me and gives you the security you say you need. That's enough for business partners to know."

"No, John, it goes beyond that. And before we sign the contract you've got to know. My sisters have had their thugs break into my home and destroy everything in it. I've had threatening phone calls, hate mail, and just about every kind of torment you can imagine."

"You sure it was them?" I asked lamely.

She looked her disgust at me and went on. Apparently, she had lived like a hermit, firing her house staff because she feared they might be bought off by her sisters. She also said she had been out when her home was ransacked but if she had been there, she would have been killed.

"I'm a little confused. If they didn't care about your father's work, why all the bad blood over the copyrights? It doesn't make sense." I'd heard of some pretty screwy family feuds but this was getting unbelievable.

"I love Daddy's work. His characters are real people to me - they're his other children. The only siblings I've got that I love are the ones my father created alone." She paused as if trying to think about how to go on so I would understand. "Because I love my brothers and because my half-sisters hate me, they will do anything to hurt me. The greatest pain they could cause is to take away all that's left of my family."

She had built to a fever pitch and was trembling. "You've got to understand, John! They're not normal; they are insane with hatred!"

I tried to console her as I thought maybe insanity was a family thing. Diana was certainly wound on a tight string. But that opinion I kept to myself. "Why don't you call them right now? Tell them the contract is signed and you're protected from them. That should get them off your back. If it will help, Sam can send an info copy of the contract to them."

"You don't understand, John, you just don't get it." She looked at me with a mixture of concern for my welfare and pity for my ignorance. "When they find out about our contract, they will try to kill you!"

I was a little shocked. I'm not usually thick headed, but if this whole deal was true, then I would be the prime target. I shook my head to clear the cobwebs and then relaxed. "Don't worry, Diana, I can handle any trouble they can bring. Call them, now." I handed her the phone.

She looked at me with a blank stare for a minute, then, flooded with relief, she dialed the numbers. As she finished the two calls, we pulled into the law offices of Twilly, Razor, and Shook.

Chapter 12

Oh for a life of sensations rather than thoughts.

~*John Keats*

Diana was a different woman after the contract was signed. She was relaxed, bright and cheerful. She seemed like life had started anew. When I asked her if she needed a ride home, she replied, "Take me to the mall, John. I want to spend some money!"

On the way, I told her she wouldn't have much time to shop because the mall closed in an hour. She assured me she didn't need much time - she knew exactly what she wanted. "I'm not going to shop, John, I'm going to buy. Then I want to go dancing." Pleadingly she asked, "Will you take me dancing? I want to paint the town red. I want to have a ball, Johnny. Please?" She was making herself giddy with excitement.

Although I took exception to being called Johnny and told her so, I told her I'd take her dancing. I was more than a little excited myself. That contract was going to do great things for my career. Her mood was contagious.

At the mall, she went straight to a Western wear store and in fifteen minutes she was a cowgirl from bandanna to boots. Everything she wore was black. High-heeled riding boots with tight black jeans made me wonder how much dancing she would manage before blisters and discomfort spoiled the mood. Her blouse was form fitting. The business suits and even the dresses I'd seen her in hid quite a lovely shape. This blouse didn't hide it - it accented her figure. The first two buttons below the collar were open and the point of the bandanna didn't come close to filling the open neck. The black outfit really set off her pale skin and blond hair.

"Well, Annie Oakley, where's your hat?" I smiled the question, still amazed at the transformation.

"Pa always said, 'The first thing a cowboy does in the morning is put on his hat, even before his gun or boots.' Maybe, before morning, I'll find a hat."

Her attitude was as unmistakable as the invitation. My first thought was she was young and over-excited. But she wasn't that young and neither was I. It was truly amazing to see the change in her.

We drove to my house so I could change clothes. I couldn't go westering in what I wore. We took the truck and started scouting the Western bars and dance halls. Diana was like a kid with a new toy. She really had a new outlook on life. We closed a couple of bars and I had to admit Diana's new boots weren't hurting her any. She danced every time the band played and drank quite a lot of wine.

Any thoughts of her as a young, impressionable girl evaporated during the first slow dance. It was a long night and we capped it off with a Mexican breakfast.

For the sake of my own conscience, I asked her which hotel she was staying at so I could take her home. She told me rather impatiently, that she had left her bag at my house and had to have it. Then she looked me right in the eyes and said, "And I've got to have you, John. Tonight! Right here in this truck, if necessary." I unbuckled her seat belt and she slid over next to me. We necked and petted our way to the house. It was almost four o'clock in the morning when we pulled up in my driveway.

She went straight up the stairs while I locked up the house and got everything turned on or off as necessary. When I got to the head of the stairs, every light in the place was on. I went into my bedroom and found her lying on the bed. She was on her side with her head propped on her hand - and naked as the day she was born!

I soon joined her.

Chapter 13

Is it not strange
That desire should so many years outlive performance?

~ *William Shakespeare, "Henry IV"*

Morning light was filtering through the curtains when I slipped out of bed. Diana was sleeping peacefully and I didn't disturb her.

Downstairs, I turned on the computer and started working. The Western mystery that I was working on was really starting to please me.

I worked steadily and became engrossed in the story that was unfolding before me. This morning, my usual pattern of writing punctuated with coffee fell apart under the constant march of words. I was in love with what I was doing. With this new story, I had passed from really pleased to engrossed to enraptured in just a few hours.

Diana offered a pleasant interruption when she came down around noon. I realized I was hungry and not just for lunch. Diana was an inspiring presence. I hated to admit it - but I couldn't deny the effect she had on me and on my writing.

She was wearing only her form-fitting, long-tailed blouse when she came into the den. She stood quietly behind me as words became sentences upon the computer screen. I soon came to a convenient stopping point, saved the document and switched off the word processor.

I don't know how her father had worked but at least she knew enough to wait patiently until I finished. There was an edge of disappointment on her face as the computer screen went blank. She concealed it poorly and asked what I was working on.

"Nothing new. Not yet, anyway."

She seemed to brighten and said she had hoped to read something I'd written this morning. I smiled at her and stood to meet her embrace.

"You can read later. Right now, I'm starved. Why don't you order us some lunch? Chinese or whatever you like. I'll make some fresh coffee." I kissed her forehead and started for the kitchen.

In the dining room, she told me pizza would be delivered in an hour. Smiling devilishly, she asked me what we could do to kill an hour. I told her we could listen to each other's stomach growl. She giggled something under her breath then took my hand and led me toward the stairs.

* * *

"I've been awake for a day and a half," I told her after we'd finished lunch. "I'm going to get some sleep."

"I need to go to the airport. Bayless and Higginbotham are leaving at four-thirty. I want to talk to them before they go." She seemed to hesitate, then asked, "Can I borrow your truck?"

I was a little surprised but too tired to be concerned. There was some reason for not calling the limo but I just didn't care. "The car's in the garage; it's more comfortable. The keys are on the table by the garage door."

"I'd prefer the truck and a way back in. We need to talk shop before I go back to Indy on Sunday."

"Same key ring. There's a door opener in the truck." I yawned and said I'd see her later.

Exhaustion and a heavy meal had their effect, I was asleep as soon as my head hit the pillow.

Chapter 14

A good indignation brings out all one's powers.

~*Ralph Waldo Emerson*

I was up shortly after midnight to start working. I was tired even though I'd been in bed for nearly ten hours. I felt like I'd been up sleep-walking, or more like sleep-running. I stretched and my shoulders ached in response.

Diana wasn't back but that didn't surprise me at all. She hadn't seemed excited or pensive when she left in the afternoon, but I was sure she got that way before she left the airport.

I put a new disc into the computer and typed the names 'Mason David and Wilson David.' These were the only two characters Hoyle had used together. They were brothers, fair and just men, strong and honest frontiersmen.

I thought about the characters and tried to recall everything about them. I had their bios - very extensive works all by themselves. As I tried to become intimately familiar with my new characters, I brought up the files on several story ideas. Nothing seemed to jump at me so I went for coffee. There was a cramp in my left hand that I hadn't noticed at the computer. The weight of the full coffee pot brought the cramp sharply into focus.

I massaged my hand under hot tap water for a few minutes. This was strange. I hadn't had hand cramps since I was in the Army. Of course, I hadn't done anything that was physically demanding since then, either. At least, nothing that demanded hand strength. Where could that cramp have come from? Or for that matter, where had this exhausted feeling come from? I felt like I used to feel after a long karate session followed by a short sleep. I hadn't worked at the martial arts since I'd left the Army Special Forces. I dried my hands; I must have just slept funny.

From the fact that my first coffee break came about thirty minutes into the night's work, I was sure this would be a typical night for me. Back at my desk, I brought up the menu of plots I'd dreamed up and never written. One of the entries drew my attention immediately.

It was a plot about a murder in a "civilized" city in the east. The plot begged for a tough, clannish, Western family to come back to solve the mystery of an old man's murder. It needed just such men as Mace and Wil David. It was perfect!

I had a sudden thought! When had I written this plot? What had been the germ of my thought process? Had it been after reading one of Hoyle's books about the David brothers? I pondered these questions for a while, then got my second cup of coffee.

I realized within minutes that I was worrying about nothing. Who cares where the idea came from? Fate had laid in my hands the perfect characters to fit my plot. I had to use what was available.

Plot and characters blended effortlessly. By six o'clock I was even more exhausted but exhilarated as well. I turned off the computer, locking the first three chapters securely in the memory of the disc.

I dumped out my unfinished second cup of coffee and went to bed.

* * *

The doorbell had rung twice. Then some persistent fool started hammering on the door. Damn! It was nine o'clock in the morning.

I got out of bed and grabbed my robe. I slipped my revolver into the robe pocket. It was a heavy Smith and Wesson .41 magnum that made my robe hang funny. But at that moment, I just didn't care. Whoever was out there was now alternately ringing the bell and beating on the door.

"I hear you and so does half of Texas!" I bellowed from the stairs. When I got to the door, I punched in the alarm code and yanked open the door. The alarm went off unexpectedly; its piercing siren startled me and I slammed the door.

I punched the alarm code again and the siren fell silent. Coming out of my daze, I remembered that Diana was supposed to have come back and I had left the alarm off. Then when I keyed in the code just now, I had activated, not deactivated, the security system. It was a careless error and I was furious with myself. I stepped back into the kitchen and called the security company to report my 'false alarm.'

The patronizing 'We understand, Mr. Noble' from the girl on the other end of the phone line made my anger worse. I was polite to her and tried to keep the sting out of my voice as I thanked her and hung up.

This whole stupid thing was the fault of whoever was outside. I made sure the alarm was off before I yanked the door open again. Diana had a key and no one else I knew would be here at this time of day. I don't know who I expected, but whoever it was, wasn't the six-foot-six-inch San Antonio police officer that was standing there.

He was trying to suppress a smile without much success. I guess he thought it was funny to see a grown man set off his own house alarm. I didn't find anything funny about it, or him. His ill-concealed mirth added to my barely controlled fury.

"Are you John Noble?" he wanted to know.

"I hope you wanted more than my name when you decided to wake me up!" I was sarcastic, tired, and angry.

"Sorry to wake you, Mr. Noble. You are John Noble, aren't you." He was patient but I could see he had to force himself to be.

"Yes, yes, officer! I'm John Noble. What do you want?"

"Is your phone number 697-8379, Mr. Noble?"

"Yes, officer...uh..." I was looking for his name tag and badge number. The bright morning sunlight was hurting my sleepy eyes and I was squinting. That made me feel inferior to this hulking cop. That feeling fueled my reckless anger.

"Sergeant, Mr. Noble. Sergeant Harold Garza. S.A.P.D. I'm investigating a homicide. I need to ask you some questions. May I come in?"

"You can show me your badge and identification papers so I can verify your story." I think I learned that from some old police show on TV, possibly Joe Friday. I needed a moment to think and verifying the sergeant's identity would give me the time. I made a mental note of the number and wrote it down next to the phone.

I was fully awake now and had a thousand questions buzzing around in my head. By the time I got through to S.A.P.D., I was scared. I didn't have many close friends and only a handful of relatives. I couldn't imagine why the police would notify me of some one's death. But Sergeant Garza was from Homicide and he was here for a reason.

The morning sun was dazzling when I opened the door to admit the homicide detective. It was hot already but that was common in this part of the country. Across the street, a couple of kids were playing in the yard. Some birds were singing and an elderly woman was heading for her mailbox. It was a beautiful morning and hard to believe someone had been murdered. Even harder to believe was that it somehow affected me.

When Sergeant Garza was seated and had refused coffee, I asked the question that I dreaded to ask. "Who was murdered?"

"I don't know, Mr. Noble. I'm hoping you can shed some light on the victim's identity. The body was found at your self-storage warehouse over on San Pedro." He could see that I was confused and was about to enlighten me when I cut him off.

"I'm not sure why you came here, Sergeant. But there are two or three murders a week in this town. I would think, with all that practice, the police could figure out who the dead man is without pestering taxpayers. Especially at this hour!"

I was fully awake and very upset. He was here because the body was on my property. There's a fence around the place that a five-year-old kid could get over - and all the customers and quite a few of my employees had keys.

"Mr. Noble. I didn't come here to bother you without a good reason." He was mad, yet he handled himself pretty well. "The victim was discovered by an electrical worker who's doing some work for you. There was no identification on the body and the worker had no idea who it was."

"The victim was wearing nothing but jeans and in one of the pockets was a scrap of paper with your phone number on it." He paused and I knew he was checking my reaction to this information. "It was your home phone number, not your business number. So, there's a strong possibility you *can* identify the body."

The body could have been anyone and having died on my property didn't mean anything. The chance of me being able to identify the corpse was very slim. Of course, that person having my home phone number probably improved the odds.

Sergeant Garza was correct in following the only lead he had, but I didn't like the interruption. I finally agreed to go to the morgue and see who this person was. I agreed mostly because I knew he could force me to do it. It just seemed better if I pretended it was alright with me.

He asked if I wanted to meet him there or to ride with him. I had no desire to spend an hour riding with him, however, Diana had my truck and Leo was sending someone to get the Cadillac for maintenance. Besides that, if Garza was going to ruin my day, he might as well have to chauffeur me around while he was doing it.

The trip to the morgue was bland. Both of us were angry and pensive. I suppose he was thinking ahead to catching the killer; I was busy with thoughts of getting home and getting some sleep. I was also thinking about Diana and the new book. She was leaving on the weekend, she had said. Well, that was a couple of days away. That was very good. She could become a habit and one that would disrupt my work. A couple more days would be perfect.

The sergeant parked in the lot and we walked into the building. As soon as I stepped through the door and felt the air-conditioned coolness, my chest tightened a little. I'd never had much association with death. I'd written of death many times - sometimes even graphically. I'd planned the deaths of dozens of characters and carried those deaths out. I had also nearly choked a soldier to death in a bar in Fayetteville, North Carolina. But that was different - I had been drunk. And besides, near death isn't death. I felt like I understood death and how it fit into the scheme of life. All life is built on death. Animals die to feed other animals. Plants die to enrich the soil for other plants. Death was a natural thing, important to the continuation of life. I still preferred to keep it at a respectful distance.

I dealt with death, fictional death, on a daily basis. However, I got an eerie, creepy feeling as I walked the sanitized halls of this building, breathed the sanitized air and saw the hard, cold faces of the men and women who worked here. These people, whose existence, like that of the building itself, depended on death, amplified the uncomfortable feeling.

There were four people sitting around what looked like a nurse's station in a hospital. Sergeant Garza interrupted their card playing and laughter. One of the men told us to wait until he finished counting his hand of cards. Garza told him we'd wait and made a joke about the man's card skills. The others laughed.

Finally, the man Garza had called Chick finished counting his points. There was a moment of boisterous conversation recapping the hand as Chick got up. He picked up a set of keys from a white, metal, glass-fronted bookcase and came into the hall with us.

"Which one of our guests are you here to visit this time, Harold?" Chick asked as we started on down the hall.

Garza gave him a number and added, "The Jane Doe that came in this morning. Mr. Noble is here to see if he can identify her." There was a small warning in the introduction. I was only guessing that it was meant for Chick to control his levity. But there was something else that bothered me more than the casual attitude.

"Garza, you just said this is a Jane Doe, but at the house, you said you had found a dead man! What's going on here?"

We started down a flight of cement stairs before he answered. "You said 'a dead man,' Mr. Noble. I just said we'd found a body."

The room we entered was even colder than the upstairs hallway had been. The tightening in my chest was choking me. There was a small table in the corner by the door and Chick picked up a clipboard. He asked Garza for the number again and turned to the right-hand wall. Along that wall were steel doors, each about three feet square. Each door had a bracket on the front for a card to be slipped into it. Most of the doors had cards in them and there were numbers scrawled on the cards.

I knew what I was seeing. I had envisioned this room - written it into existence, yet seeing it, actually looking at those cold, steel doors, startled me. Chick opened one of the doors and reached inside to pull the sliding table out into the light.

"Please come over here, Mr. Noble. Can you identify the lady?"

The tightening in my chest doubled, then doubled again. I was choking and lights were flashing in front of my eyes. Then darkness, soft, silky darkness engulfed me. I felt hands on me, then something cold on my face.

* * *

I was sitting in a chair with the world swimming around me. There was a bitter tinge in my nostrils; I knew it was the residue from smelling salts. I had fainted.

I shook my head to clear it and squeezed my eyes shut. When I opened them, I glanced over at the dead lady on the slab. Again I trembled and the world wavered. Garza was talking to me. I had no idea what he was saying. His words penetrated the fog of my brain but the meanings were lost. He swung his right hand up toward my face; I thought he was going to hit me. I jumped before realizing his hand was moving slowly, then the pungent sting of the smelling salts was in my nose again.

The world came into sharp focus. Garza was asking if I was alright. Chick was holding me in the chair and pressing a cold towel to my head. The sterile room gleamed white and silver in the cold, fluorescent light. The woman's body lay with the head and shoulders exposed.

It was Diana!

Chapter 15

A vague uneasiness; the police. It's like when you suddenly understand you have to undress in front of the doctor.

~Ugo Betti

Garza drove me home. The afternoon sun was bright. I noted the congestion on the freeway, but only that it was there. In about an hour, at five, it would be much worse.

Diana was dead! I still couldn't believe it. She had felt so secure since we'd signed the contract. The thought of that contract brought me a twinge. I was now the sole owner of those copyrights. It felt funny to think of that.

Garza had told me that Diana's body was discovered by one of my contractors. She was wearing only her black jeans and had no identification. She had been strangled, Garza said, and maybe raped. I doubted the rape. It wasn't logical that the killer would have put her pants back on her. Garza told me the coroner had found semen in her but no other physical evidence of rape. I explained that the semen was probably mine.

I'd spent most of the day at the morgue and at Sergeant Garza's office. I told him everything I knew about her in as much detail as I could. As I watched him write his report, I realized all I knew about Diana wasn't very much.

Finally, satisfied that he knew all I could tell him, Garza put his paperwork away and we left his office. That seemed like days ago instead of just fifteen minutes.

At the curb where Diana's limo had always stopped, Garza pulled up. He didn't turn off the car, just shifted into the parking gear.

"Here's my card, Mr. Noble. You've been a big help and I appreciate it. If you can think of anything else, no matter how small, give me a call." The animosity between us had disappeared. Garza seemed like a good man and a good cop. Good enough, in fact, to cause me to apologize for my verbal onslaught earlier.

I laid his card on the foyer table and went to the liquor cupboard. I needed a drink in the worst way. I poured the last of my Scotch into a shot glass. About half of a shot is all there was and that wasn't anywhere near enough.

I went to the garage to get a new bottle. I was shocked to find my truck parked in the garage! I struggled to fight down panic as the meaning of it being there hit me. Diana had driven the truck, and she was dead, and the truck was in my garage.

I forgot the Scotch and ran back into the house. The panic was rising as I called Sam Twilly. He was just about to leave but his secretary caught him.

"Calm down, John. I'll be right over. Call the homicide detective and tell him to come back. I'm on my way. Just calm down!"

Garza arrived first. When I let him in, he asked if I had remembered something. I hadn't told him why I wanted him to come back - just that it was important to the case.

I told him he'd have to wait. I wanted Sam to be present because this looked like it would make me the prime suspect. He was getting irritated with my stalling by the time Sam rang the bell.

After cursory introductions, I explained, "Sergeant Garza, my truck is in the garage. I discovered it there just after you dropped me off. I haven't touched it - I didn't want to mess anything up for you."

"Why the lawyer, Mr. Noble? Do you think you need him?" Garza had jumped to the conclusion that I was about to confess.

I took a long breath to settle my nerves. "There's a pretty damning piece of evidence in my garage. I don't know how it got there, but there it is. If you mean do I need my lawyer because I'm guilty, the answer is no! However, I pay Mr. Twilly to look out for my legal interests and to protect my rights - so yes, I need him."

"Sergeant Garza," Sam added, "Mr. Noble wouldn't have called you or left the vehicle for your examination if he had anything to hide. I suggest we go look at the evidence."

Garza agreed and we trooped down the hallway to the garage door. The detective went in while Sam and I stayed in the doorway and kept out of his way.

Garza, careful not to touch anything, looked through the open passenger's window. "The keys are in the ignition," he reported. He moved around the front of the truck and passed his hand just above the hood. "Feels cool." He looked through the driver's window without comment. He was looking at the truck and the garage floor and everything else, it seemed.

"Mr. Noble, come here, but be careful not to touch anything." He was looking into the bed of the truck as he spoke.

I walked around beside him. He was staring at a bundle of clothes - a blouse, a cowboy hat, and a pair of cowgirl boots. The little bundle was against the passenger's side of the bed and couldn't be seen from the house door where Sam and I waited. My breathing became a little erratic. They were Diana's clothes!

"Those her things?" he asked.

"Those are her clothes. She just bought them the night before last."

Garza said, "So far everything indicates Mrs. Faire was a modest dresser. I wonder why such an otherwise conservative woman would buy such an obnoxious hat." His disgust with the gaudy Stetson was obvious. I could also tell he was trying to find something psychological, if not sinister, in her having the hat.

He had to be set straight. "That's my hat." I tried to make it just a statement of fact but he seemed to think I was defending that damned eyesore. I hated that hat and he certainly hadn't offended me. I tried to clarify by explaining that Diana hadn't bought a hat. "She must have taken this one from my closet when she went to the airport."

The same sinister implication came through when he said, "Whether she bought it or not, she wore it. That still doesn't fit with the general image of the woman." He was talking aloud but his comments were for his own benefit. He was busy trying to figure if my statements about her general image were misleading or if there was something diabolical in her death that the hat might point to. He said he had to call the lab to come examine the evidence.

The police lab moved into my garage in force. They poked and prodded everything in there. They dusted for fingerprints, looked for tears in the upholstery, checked for blood, hair, and who knows what else.

They spent the better part of six hours sprinkling, spraying, powdering, taping, taking pictures, and, in general, examining the evidence. Sergeant Garza spent most of that time on the phone. He was dictating reports, collecting information and talking to his partner. There were two uniformed policemen covering the neighborhood and asking questions of all my neighbors. Police work had come a long way since Sherlock Holmes and Joe Friday.

Sam stayed with me in the kitchen. We hovered around the coffee pot and Sam made phone calls in the rare moments when Garza wasn't on the line. For the most part, I just sat and drank coffee. I was exhausted but too keyed up to sleep. Occasionally, Sam or I would slip out to the garage to see what was going on, then come right back to be out of the way.

After one such foray, Sam came back and sat down. "That's *your* hat?" He sounded astonished.

I smiled at him. "Ugliest damned thing you ever saw, ain't it?"

Sam tried to be polite but we both knew I was right. I hated that hat. Harriet had gotten some specialty shop to make it for me. It was a surprise gift - surprise, all right, and the most miserable surprise I'd ever gotten.

Harriet didn't understand the true cowboy ideal and it showed in that gift. Cowboys were moral, simple, sensible creatures. They lived in a harsh, often hostile, land. Their life demanded going about the countryside in an inconspicuous manner. Nothing flashy or shiny was worn because it could draw unwanted attention. In the old West, there was usually a shortage of clothing. Many folks wore what they could make for themselves. Sometimes, a young cowboy, if he could afford it, would have a 'town suit' that had some flash and flare to it. They would use the special garb for the infrequent trips to 'paint the town.' But even the flashiest, for-the-whorehouse hats paled beside that monstrosity Harriet had given me.

If she had read any of my books, she would have known better. I tried to live the cowboy lifestyle as far as attitude and appearance. I fell short of my standards, but I could never have worn that travesty in felt. I had never put it on my head.

Harriet and I had a terrible fight when she gave it to me. I had made fun of the hat and her taste. I guess she had really tried to be nice, but...

Sam was still astonished. "I can't imagine you owning such a thing and I certainly can't picture Diana wearing it."

"Harriet gave me that sickly thing about a year before we were divorced. The fight we had over me refusing to wear it was pretty bad. She would probably have killed me if I had thrown it away. And, believe me, that's what I wanted to do with it. As a peaceful gesture, I put it in the closet on a separate hat rack. I made it sound like it was a special place of honor in the closet." Thinking of that hat still makes me shudder. "I haven't seen that hat since I put it in the closet - until tonight.

"When Diana bought her Western duds, I asked about a hat. She told me she'd find a hat by morning. I didn't even know she had taken it."

Ponderingly, I added, "But, you're right Sam. I can't believe she wore it. She must have been quite a spectacle at the airport."

Harriet called and interrupted the only comfortable conversation Sam and I had been able to have all evening. She asked what the police were doing at my house. The police cars and the lab trucks had undoubtedly drawn the interest of the neighborhood and unquestionably sent Vivian into a frenzy. I didn't feel like talking to Harriet and I didn't owe her any answers.

Without saying a word, I handed the phone to Sam. He diplomatically, politely told Harriet to mind her own business. He could scold someone and make them want to thank him for it. I was sure glad he was on my side.

Sam talked to me in exhaustive speeches punctuated by phone calls and coffee. He was alternately trying to fill me in on what the police knew or didn't know, and trying to keep my confidence up.

Around nine o'clock, the two uniformed officers reported to Garza and talked for about twenty minutes. I could see them in the dining room but couldn't hear what they were saying. Between the three of them, they had made pages of notes.

About three hours later the lab crew huddled in the garage. Two of them started putting up their equipment while three others started cleaning up the mess they had made. The last fellow went to Sergeant Garza and started the debriefing. By half past midnight, everyone was gone but Garza and Sam.

We sat in the dining room over coffee. Garza told me he wanted me to go to Police Headquarters the next day to have my fingerprints recorded. "The dead woman's prints are there and hundreds of prints that I'm sure are yours. There are some small prints, kid-sized, and one other set of adult prints. The other set is on the steering wheel, the keychain, door handle and the control for the garage door opener."

"My prints should be on file from my time in the army," I said.

"Could those other prints be the killer's?" Sam wanted to know.

"Could be, but I doubt it." Then he looked at me and asked, "Where's your car, Mr. Noble?"

I hadn't even thought about the car. "It's in the shop for maintenance. What does that have to do with anything?"

"One of your neighbors says she saw someone move the truck out of the driveway, take out the car, and then put the truck in the garage. She said the man looked to be about fifty, medium build and height. Any ideas?"

"Sounds like Leo Donaldson. He's my business manager. He was supposed to pick up the car and take it to the shop. I usually park the truck out of the way so he can get the car without any problems. I guess the killer left the truck in the way."

"I want this Donaldson to go downtown for fingerprints, also. What's his address?" He scribbled down Leo's address as I gave it to him. "Mr. Noble, you understand you're a suspect in this murder. So's Donaldson!"

"Are you planning to arrest my client, Sergeant?" Sam came to his feet and stood ready.

"No, Mr. Twilly, at least, not yet. But he is a suspect and I wanted him to know that." Then he looked at me and continued, "Don't plan any vacations or business trips any time soon, Mr. Noble. Your fainting scene this morning was real, but I have to look at things objectively. Did you faint from surprise or fear of discovery? You have immediate access to the scene of the murder in your garage. That woman had your private phone number in her pocket. You're a suspect."

I'll say this for Garza, he didn't pull his punches. He left after reminding me to call Leo and to go for fingerprints.

At two in the morning, Sam left and I was worn out.

Chapter 16

Divorce is a game played by lawyers.

~*Cary Grant*

This hammering at the door in the morning hours was getting old. I was heavy with sleep and Scotch when I yanked the door open. "What do you want?" I demanded of the Bexar County deputy sheriff standing on my front step.

"Are you John Noble?" he asked politely. His presence and manner reminded me of when I was served the papers telling me Harriet had counter-sued in the divorce proceedings. My first thought was that this guy was here to arrest me for Diana's murder. That didn't make any sense; the city police were investigating the murder - why would the county sheriff be coming to arrest me?

"Deputy, if you don't know who the hell I am, why are you beating on my door?" I fixed him with my best evil glare, but it didn't work.

He just simply asked again, "Are you John Noble?"

"Yes, I'm John Noble, now what do you want?" I was belligerent and spoiling for a fight. Of course, when I simmered down, I'd know I didn't want to start a fight with a deputy sheriff. But right at that moment, I was mad, tired, and still a little drunk.

He handed me an envelope and said, "This is for you, sir. Have a nice day." Then he turned and walked away.

I screamed a curse at his retreating back but he was a professional and refused to rise to the bait. He just continued down the sidewalk and then drove off in his squad car.

I slumped down at my desk and tore open the envelope. There was a neat stack of legal documents inside. I slid them out and started wading through the legal chatter that was there. By the time I'd read through the first page, I'd figured out the message even without knowing all of the words. Harriet had filed a temporary custody restraining order so I couldn't see the kids for a while.

I was trembling with rage as I dialed her number. The phone rang four times and the answering machine got my call. I slammed the phone down; I didn't want to talk to a stupid machine.

I didn't want to talk to Harriet either - I wanted to strangle her!

I picked up the phone again and pushed the redial button. I reminded myself, while I waited for the answering machine, that I had to speak carefully because if I said anything rash, Harriet would find a convenient, innocent way to make sure kids heard the message. "Harriet," I told the machine, "this is John. Call me." I laid the receiver back in the cradle.

There was no sense in calling Sam and screaming. These papers had been served and until he saw them, he couldn't do anything about them. I also knew that no matter how big a tantrum I threw, he wouldn't go to the courthouse until everything was right. I paid him to be that painstaking but sometimes it galled me.

I'd had enough sleep. I took a shower and ate breakfast. When I felt like I'd sobered up and calmed down, I grabbed the envelope and headed for the garage.

As soon as I saw the truck, I wondered if I was supposed to move it, or even touch it. Garza hadn't said. Oh, well, he hadn't said not to use it and I needed transportation.

I drove to Sam's office to drop off the legal package. I knew he would be busy but his secretary would be sure he knew I had been there. Once Sam saw the restraining order, he'd know what to do and would do it.

Sam's secretary quickly made a copy of the whole package as she explained that Sam was in a very important conference. I didn't figure I'd see him and that was just as well. I had other business to attend to this afternoon. She assured me he would see it as soon as his meeting broke up.

I drove to the little brick office building on Marbach Road that was my corporate headquarters. Leo was sitting behind his desk with a drink in his hand. I think that was the first time I'd ever seen him drink hard liquor and I knew it was the first time I'd seen him drink at the office. He jumped up as I came in. I waved him back to his seat but he stood anyway.

"I guess you've heard, Leo," I said as I took a seat in the leather side chair. "We've got to go give the coppers our fingerprints."

"John, I'm scared." He came around the desk and sat on the other side chair. His hands were shaking and his eyes told a story of a lot of drinking in a short period. He didn't seem to be drunk, but everything indicated he had been at the bottle since early morning. He finished the drink in his hand before he continued. "John, I'm scared. I know this is pretty selfish, John, but damnit, I'm scared." His eyes were hollow and he'd aged quite a bit in the week since I'd last seen him. I wondered how much of that age had come to him in the last few hours. I wasn't sure what was so frightening but something was riding him hard. Had he killed Diana? Is that what was churning him up? That was a ridiculous thought. I was getting jumpy.

"Leo, I don't know what you're afraid of but it can't be as bad as you're making it out to be. Tell me what's eating you."

He got up and poured himself another drink. I started to tell him to lay off the sauce, then thought better of it. Leo had never told me much about his personal life and whenever the conversation drifted that way he changed the subject. He always did it abruptly enough to send a clear signal that his personal life was personal. He had never been rude - just obvious and firm. I didn't figure he'd be very receptive to being told he was drinking too much. Besides that, I was scared and I'd spent my time in a Scotch bottle last night. I guess Leo had as much right to drink away his fears as I did. Although for the life of me, I couldn't begin to imagine what he was so scared of.

He took his drink and went to the window. He stood there staring out into the early afternoon sunshine. Dust motes danced in the shaft of sunlight that flooded around him. After a few minutes, he turned, sipped his drink. He seemed to have gained some self control and said, "I'm thoroughly ashamed of what I'm about to say, John. But I've got to say it." He downed his drink.

"John, I read about the murder in the paper this morning. The detectives were here before nine asking all sorts of questions. John, you're in trouble - deep trouble. I'm worried 'bout you."

I cut him off and told him not to worry. "Maybe I'm an idealist, Leo, but I didn't kill that girl. That's got to count for something. Hell, man, I was enjoying having her around."

"I'm a realist, John. And I'm real worried about me." He was staring at the carpet. He cleared his throat and went on. His face was dark red and it wasn't just the bourbon. "John, I'm worried about you going to jail. I like you and you've been good to me. Real good! That's why I'm so worked up. For forty years I lived from payday to payday. Then you came along and I started making money like I never had before. You made me foreman and then your business manager. I'm not rich but I'm better off than I ever was before. That's the kind of thing you can grow used to real easy.

"I know you're real busy with all you do and I run the company. I kind of feel like a tycoon sometimes. Like the wheeling and dealing is for my own company instead of yours. Don't get me wrong, John. I don't mean I'd do you dirty or nothing like that but I do feel like it's mine sometimes."

He looked me right in the eye. He was a proud man but very embarrassed at the moment. "John, I have to admit the biggest part of my concern for you is what going to jail would do to this company and to my job. I'm sorry, John, but that's the truth and I thought you should know. I'm sorry."

I wanted to laugh at such a petty concern but I had to deal carefully with his emotions. I also had to remember it was only petty to me. To him it was a very real problem. I stared into the carpet for a second. "Leo, pour me a drink and then sit your butt down."

"First of all," I told him when I had my drink, "I'm not going to jail. Second and most important, this business goes on like always. Hell, I go months at a time without ever thinking about this operation. It would be just the same if I went to jail."

"When I promoted you to business manager, I gave you ten percent of the business because I wanted you to feel like it was your company - and to have a stake in the outcome." I drank my drink. "Regardless of the outcome, you're here to stay. Period."

He seemed greatly relieved, then even more embarrassed than before. He also felt sorry for his selfish attitude. It didn't bother me because I was innocent and the killer would be found. I'm also very self-centered but I don't resent that same quality in others. Especially not in people I liked and respected. Leo Donaldson was certainly one of those people.

Although Leo seemed to be in control of himself, I didn't know how much he'd had to drink. And, if it was as much as I suspected, I didn't want him behind the wheel of a car. I drove us downtown. During the ride, he talked freely, intermixing excessive, sincere apologies with routine business chat. Except for the pleas for forgiveness, he was his old self again in every way.

Leo and I had both been fingerprinted by the military, but we submitted to the ritual again. After we'd been fingerprinted, I tried to find Garza but he was out. Leo and I left the police station and stopped for supper on the way back to the office. I left Leo at the office; he said he wanted to catch up on some paperwork. All I wanted was a little Scotch and a lot of sleep.

I tried to work after midnight but nothing worthwhile came of the effort. I did some home chores and idled away the hours 'til dawn. My whole purpose was to try to get back on my schedule. I was sure that when my routine came back so would everything else.

Chapter 17

I feel bad that I don't feel worse.

~*Michael Frayn*

I woke at one in the afternoon fully refreshed and ready to work. I usually spent the afternoon hours doing writing business paperwork. I attacked the neglected stack of mail with forced enthusiasm. This was the part of my business life that I dreaded, but it had to be done. I consoled myself that I was back on my schedule, and that idea made the drudgery bearable. The truth was I still hated the task but fooling myself with trifling goals and rewards was easy. The only business that I handled was the business associated with my writing. I thought of Leo. One of the basic reasons I had hired him was so I wouldn't have to suffer this kind of drudgery for any of my other enterprises. It still amazed me that he hadn't seen how important he was to the company. If he only knew how I hated doing the kind of work he did for me, he'd feel exceedingly secure. He'd probably even ask for a raise.

I realized I was woolgathering instead of working.

There was a thank you card from Chucky. He enjoyed his visit but was glad to be back at home and at work. There was also a thank you card from Mrs. Cooper for the flowers I'd sent her.

I hadn't touched the mail in over a week and there was a ton of it. I just threw away the junk mail. The obvious bills I stacked aside for later. There was a bundle of fan mail that my publisher had forwarded. I amused myself with that for an hour or so. I always enjoyed the ego boost that stuff gave me. I never answered it, but I always read it.

My vanity satisfied, I decided to work on my hunger. I made myself a nice brunch and went out to get the paper. The last two days' papers were there. I should have thrown the day-old paper out like day-old bread, but I didn't. The first thing I saw was a banner headline proclaiming Diana's death. My mood turned bad with the headline and grew worse as I read the curt article that followed.

PUBLISHING HEIRESS MURDERED

"Police Thursday were investigating the strangulation death of a woman. The partly nude body was found on the city's northwest side behind a self-storage warehouse.

Investigators say the woman, now identified as Diana Sue Faire, was choked to death late Wednesday night. They were not sure if she had been raped. The medical examiner is conducting an autopsy.

Faire, of Indianapolis, was here on business. Police say local businessman John Noble is the chief suspect in the murder but refused further comments. No arrests have been made."

There was more but I threw the paper down. How could Diana have been murdered and why was I being implicated? My brunch had lost its zest after the two inches of newsprint. I didn't even bother going back to the paperwork. Anger and frustration were fighting for control of my mental process. Desperation and depression had won their battle for my physical ability. I just sat at the kitchen table unmoving, uncaring and unable to think.

A few hours later I got up and got the Scotch. Why did all of this have to happen when things were starting to go right. By six in the evening, I was as drunk as a skunk. That's a stupid saying; I'd never seen a drunk skunk. Where do all these silly sayings come from? I remembered thinking about that as I poured the last of the Scotch from the bottle. I also remembered thinking that I'd just opened that bottle twenty-four hours ago. It worried me to realize I'd drank so much in so short a time.

I thought of Leo.

During my divorce, I'd drank way too much. I wondered if I was an alcoholic. Harriet had taken away the kids then, too.

This was too much for me. I couldn't focus on anything. The world was buzzing and spinning. I couldn't escape the noise or the swirling collage of faces. The phone rang; I could see Diana. The refrigerator kicked on; I saw Harriet. The clock chimed; the twins' faces flashed at me. Vivian was talking over the fence in a voice that sounded like traffic noise at rush hour.

The stairs were too steep and they were moving. I slept on the living room floor.

* * *

Sunday morning was unusually cool, gray, and drizzly. I woke up with a hangover and a bad mood. I was suffering from a feeling of persecution. Strangely, I didn't think about Diana or the cruel death she'd suffered. I also didn't believe I'd be convicted, or even charged with her murder. I was brooding about the interruptions to my work and my privacy.

I suddenly thought of Harriet's lawyer calling me spoiled. Thinking of him always upset me. He was a viper making a living by convincing distraught women that their plight was worse than it actually had been and that they were entitled to much greater retribution for their patient suffering. My shrink said I've transferred the blame for the divorce to that shyster.

I lit a cigarette and went to my desk.

Forty-five minutes later I shut off the computer without having written a word. I took a glass of Scotch and went outside on the patio. I spent an hour bitterly hating lawyers. I devised a dozen plots out of my daydreams about how to eliminate lawyers from the face of the earth. Every bad thing that had ever happened to me had a lawyer connected with it. Damn!

Thinking of plots built from daydreams made me realize, or rationalize, that I was working - in a sort of an off-key way. I left my empty glass on the patio table and went into the house.

After a long, hot shower, I went back to the computer and worked for six straight hours. What I wrote wasn't the best, but not too bad. With some serious edits, it would be worthwhile. I went to the bedroom to lay down and rest.

Just after I lay down, the phone rang. I let the machine answer it, but when I heard Sam start to leave a message, I grabbed the phone.

Sam didn't count as a lawyer because he was a friend and he was honest. I held none of my lawyer-animosity toward him. "Sam, I'm here. What's going on?"

"John, I'm glad you're there. We need to get together tomorrow. Can you come to my office at eleven?"

I had an idea what we needed to meet about, yet I was a little irritated at another schedule interruption. But, Sam wouldn't call without good reason. I spoke calmly, "Sure. I can be there. What's Harriet up to?

"She's up to no good as I'm sure you figured, but we'll talk about that later. There are more pressing matters, John."

Confused, I asked, "If tomorrow isn't about Harriet, then what's the meeting for?

"It's about the murder, John." He sounded a bit frustrated and went on. "I've retained Chris Taravella to represent you. He's a top-notch criminal attorney and ..."

"I'm not guilty!" I almost yelled as I interrupted him. "Damnit, Sam. What do I need a criminal lawyer for?"

Sam was quiet for a moment then said softly. "I sometimes think you need a nanny. You're so naive I must continually remind myself that you are an adult." He took a deep breath. "John, please listen to me. You need a criminal lawyer because you're going to be arrested for a crime - a very serious crime. Hang innocence! I know you're innocent - but you're going to be arrested. Once you accept that reality, you can move on to saving yourself."

I was stunned. Sam had never been insulting. I didn't know what to make of it. And I didn't know why he was so sure I'd be arrested. And I didn't know why I needed another damned lawyer in my life. When I asked, he explained in his old patient manner.

"John you're a conscientious writer - a real professional. You always send out only the work you think is ready. Right?"

"Yeah, but what's that got to do with being arrested and more lawyers?"

"About three years ago we had lunch and you were very poor company. Do you recall? We were at one of those all-day breakfast places you like so well. While I held up my end of the conversation, you had your nose buried in the current issue of some news magazine. You were complaining about an article of yours in that issue."

He continued coaxing me into the memory, but he didn't need to. I remembered only too well. Chucky had cut a deal with the magazine for me to write three articles. I got sidetracked with my novel and forgot the articles. Chucky called to bug me because we were about to miss the deadline. I rushed out the first article in two days. When I mailed it to Chucky, I was satisfied with it. When the publisher sent my courtesy copies and I read what I'd written, I was embarrassed and dismayed. I was surprised they had even printed it. Chucky, Sam, and Leo had all said it was a good article but my standards were too high. I had lunch with Sam the next day.

"What does that have to do with this, Sam? The article stunk, but nobody will arrest me for that."

I knew from his irritation earlier that this was very obvious to him and probably everyone else on planet Earth so I tried not to be too dense. Sam patiently continued, "John, there are a lot more murders in this town than there are cops to solve them. The detective will start out with every intention of getting to the truth …"

"And we both know where the road paved with good intentions leads to. Don't we?" I interrupted. He agreed and I thought: it leads to more lawyers.

"The police captain will start badgering the detective to wrap up the Faire case and get on to the next one. The evidence against you is pretty solid and the more the captain yells, the more the detective will be sure that the evidence is right. Just as you were so sure that article was the way you wanted it while your agent was yelling about the deadline.

"I don't think for a minute that Garza would take the easy way out. Just as you wouldn't send out an article that didn't meet your standards. Do you understand?"

I understood and grunted.

"You will be arrested, John. When you go to jail, the press is going to latch onto the story in a big way."

"Why? If there are so many killings, why will this one be so special?" I don't think I'm overly stupid but I couldn't see things quite the way Sam did.

"Because, John, you're a man of wealth. With you as the suspect, and this looking like a murder-for-money, there will be plenty of stink. In the newspaper business, plenty of stink means plenty of ink. You'll look like a big fish trying to get bigger. The death clause in the contract will hurt you. It provides a motive. You live an eccentric lifestyle, and there are plenty of people who would be glad to tell the reporters about it - like Harriet, for example. Even if she didn't intentionally do so, she's just no match for high-pressure journalists.

"The press will sell a lot of papers on those two issues alone. The average guy who reads the paper is an average-income kind of guy trying hard to get ahead. And he reads about you - a man with a lot of money and a lot of business interests. The papers say you are suspected of killing Diana for more money and this average guy gets pissed. It offends his sense of justice. The more press coverage you get, the less chance you have of getting a jury that isn't tainted by the headlines. Your best bet for a fair trial, if it comes to that," he paused and corrected himself, "when it comes to that, is to stay out of jail."

"Alright, Sam! I'm convinced, but what do I do?" I was feeling the panic rise. My throat was dry and there was a funny taste in my mouth.

"Let Taravella handle it. He can keep you out of jail. That's important! But I'm not the one to talk to. Meet me here at eleven and don't worry."

"I'll be there," I told him before I dropped the phone back on the hook.

Life is never simple when there are people in it. I lay back on the bed and thought of how many times I'd written that thought. Always before, I'd used it in context with one of my Western heroes, usually a mountain man. For such a person, life was simple in theory - difficult in practice - but very simple in theory. Those fellows were alone; they had nobody to depend on. To eat meant to hunt. To stay warm meant to gather fuel. To do either meant to study nature. They had no time for woolgathering and interpersonal relationships. Living was a day-to-day struggle - a battle fought against nature. But unlike all other women, Mother Nature was a simple creature.

Why were these people my favorite characters? Were they my heroes? Did I long for the simple life I built for them? Did I build that simple life for them so I could escape into it myself? Did such a simple life only exist in my imagination? Did I create it just for the benefit of my heroes?

I had a theory about heroes. Everybody needs heroes to serve as role models for some aspect of their lives. But most people don't understand their own definitions of the role models they create. At least, not until they can discuss those ideas with other people who know about that particular hero. The other people don't have to agree with your definition or even the attributes you see in your hero. All the other person has to do is provide intelligent conversation. Any point they make - pro or con - helps you clearly define the attribute you wish to achieve.

I fell asleep while I was trying to decide if I built my characters into heroes so I could discuss them, or if I built them to live the life I wanted for myself.

As I slept, my heroes stood silently guarding my slumber and on this night there were some new guardians.

Some of Hoyle's heroes were there.

Chapter 18

A wise man always throws himself on the side of his assailants. It is more his interest than it is theirs to find his weak point.

~Ralph Waldo Emerson

Sam and I left his office for the short drive to Taravella's just after eleven. By noon we were entangled in legal wrangling with San Antonio's consummate criminal attorney. Chris Taravella was a small man. He stood about five-two and probably didn't weigh a hundred pounds. I couldn't tell if he was thirty or fifty-five, but I was sure he was between those ages. What little hair he had was black as night but very thin and fine. At first glance, his head just looked dirty. His frail hands looked almost feminine in form but were covered with scars - like the hands of a bare-knuckle fighter. There was such a contrast in the form and function of his hands that I found myself distracted - almost daydreaming. I wondered how such a contrast would come about.

His voice was well trained. That's the best description I can give. At times it was cultured, refined, powerful. At others it was soothing; still harsh at other times. Always, there seemed a reason for the change. He seemed to be able to take in the entire room at a sleepy glance. He noticed my frequent distractions and always brought me back to the import of the discussion. But he always did so in such a way that I never felt truculent.

We discussed all of the evidence and all of the plausible ways that such evidence could have come to be. Frankly, it didn't sound very encouraging, even to me.

I was also starting to wonder about me. I was facing a death sentence - or, at best, life in prison. I should be scared stiff but my mind kept wandering. Was I just a callous man or too stupid to see the gravity of the situation?

Taravella started over. Every fact, every theory, every opinion. He scrubbed the case from various angles. His secretary recorded everything.

It was obvious to me that he intended to know everything, to commit it to memory so he could mix and match the parts to see if a new theory came forward.

He continued and I answered questions from rote. I realized he was preparing me for the trial, if necessary. My mind wandered as we droned on. I realized I had complete confidence in this man. I tried to explain why I felt that way but lost concentration.

His office was beautiful. Dark walnut paneling covered all three exposed walls. The fourth wall, the one behind his desk, was an enormous, floor-to-ceiling bookcase. The outer wall held two tall picture windows concealed by closed mini-blinds and curtains. The furnishings were massive. He had a large walnut desk, neatly scattered with open law books and legal pads. There was a heavy brown sofa against one wall; the matching side chairs were in front of the windows.

Taravella sat in a high backed, roller chair behind his desk. His secretary was at a computer desk to his right. She hadn't said a word in the hours we'd been there, but no word had been spoken that she hadn't entered into the computer.

Sam sat on the side chair nearest the desk. His elbows were on the arms of the chair and his hands were folded, choirboy style, in front of his face.

I sat on the sofa.

It was past five o'clock when we left and I felt drained. I was asleep by six and up just after midnight. I worked on the David brothers and a bottle of Scotch. I had more success with the bottle than I did with the brothers for the first few hours.

The blue light from the computer screen stared blankly at me! I reached to turn it off when a sudden thought struck me. Those heroes standing guard over my sleep with unfailing diligence inspired some coherent thought. What if they failed? What if I lost them? What would happen to me?

What if I gave them away ... like Diana had?

I started linking some crazy thoughts together. They fell in place very easily. There was a storyline in this somewhere. I cleared the screen and started working on it.

I worked effortlessly for seven hours. I shut off the computer and dragged myself up the stairs. Without undressing, I fell across the bed wide awake.

My brain was fuzzy but I kept thinking. And I didn't like the thoughts! I couldn't concentrate on Diana's murder. I tried being one of my fictional sleuths but I ended up on a thousand other thoughts. Who did kill Diana? Why? I just couldn't follow those thoughts. Why?

Thinking about my defense wasn't any better. My conscious mind simply wouldn't hold still on that matter. I found myself rationalizing that since I couldn't figure out who did it, I couldn't defend myself against all of the unknowns. I did, however, figure out why I trusted Taravella - it was simpler than worrying about how to defend myself. Just that! It was the lazy man's way out.

Or the coward's?

My only prolonged train of thought was on work. But I was unhappy with that. In the past week, I'd started three major novels. I felt like I couldn't concentrate on one for any period of time. I was mentally wafted away by transient thoughts.

Somewhere in this muddle of thoughts, sleep came. I gladly fell into the slumber, even knowing it too was an emotional escape from reality.

Chapter 19

The mob has many heads but no brains.

~Thomas Fuller

My alarm clock startled me when it rang. I shut it off and tried to recall why I had set it. It was one o'clock in the afternoon. I'd had about three hours sleep and I was groggy. On the way to the kitchen for coffee, I remembered that Matt Brown was coming to see me at two o'clock.

Coffee first, a shower, and then whatever happened I could handle.

"I'm afraid you're not getting your money's worth on this case, Mr. Noble." Matthew Brown was a man of fifty. He looked like a military officer without a uniform. He was prim and erect as if he had just left West Point. I knew he had been an Army officer for nearly thirty years. Now, Matt Brown was in a very different line of work; he certainly didn't look like a private investigator.

He looked so little like a private eye that when I had built the main character for my Hermon Press mysteries, I had taken Matt Brown as my sample detective. Taken him, that is, and listed every important characteristic of the man. I changed everything on the list to its opposite pole. I even made Hermon physically opposite to Matt. At one extreme is Matt Brown and at the other extreme is Hermon Press. The only common cord was efficient, accurate, and professional investigation.

I had used Matt a couple of times before for both business and personal issues. I liked the way he worked and the results he got. Just after Diana was murdered, I called him and put him to work on it. This was our first face-to-face meeting since he had started on the case.

"There are just too many people looking into this case. At the airport, I found out that Miss Faire arrived alone, met Mr. Higginbotham and Mr. Bayless at Gate 25. After the two men boarded their plane, she left alone. I also found out the city police and two other private investigating firms had been there before me."

"At the hotel, I was ahead of the police but the private forces had already been there and they were different people than those at the airport." He consulted his notebook, "I count at least five separate, unofficial investigations going on, not including my own."

"Who's hiring all of these gumshoes?" I wanted to know.

His look was one of irritation mixed with understanding. He didn't like the term "gumshoe" and felt like I included him in that group. He was still, mentally, an Army officer and he somewhat expected people to speak to him as subordinates speak to *the* Colonel. He accepted my comment silently because he also understood he wasn't my Colonel; he was on my payroll - he was my gumshoe. His voice showed none of the irritation that was in his face. "I can't say for sure in all cases. A couple of women in Arizona have hired Marc Jones. He's good; I don't have a line on the women, but Jones is good. Harry Kelsey said something about 'his people in Wisconsin' being interested. I don't know who in Wisconsin, but somebody. The others are unknowns. Marc and Harry don't know either."

"I may know who the Wisconsin people are," I told him, "and the old ladies in Arizona are Diana's half-sisters." What I wanted to know was who else was so deeply interested in the case. And why!

"Mind telling me who it is in Wisconsin? It may help fill in the gaps." Matt Brown was thorough and he collected every tidbit of information on any case he was handling.

I was sure it wouldn't help him any and I only thought I knew, but I told him I suspected my publisher of doing the hiring. I couldn't imagine why they would get involved or even care, but they were the only people I knew in Wisconsin. Of course, Diana might have had contacts there who would be interested. I also told him Higginbotham likely had someone in the field. He made a few notes and started to leave.

He stopped in the foyer and added, "Mr. Noble, there's one other thing about this case that is strange. Usually, people don't want to get involved, witnesses conveniently don't remember or just refuse to talk, that sort of thing. This case is different. I don't know exactly why but people whom I'm sure would not want to 'get involved' in other cases are volunteering information on this one. That may be good for you, or it may muddy the waters. I thought you should know."

"What makes Diana's murder so different, Matt?"

"Like I said, I don't really know why. The press is having a ball with it. She was a beautiful woman. I could see that from the big picture they put in the paper. It's going to be a hard time for you, one way or the other."

"Thanks, Matt. I need a few more problems." He knew I was glad he told me in spite of my grumbling remark. "Who removed the body from the morgue?"

"It's being moved tomorrow afternoon. Mr. Higginbotham made all of the arrangements by phone. The body goes to a funeral home over on Main Street and into a very expensive casket. Very expensive! Then it goes to the airport. Mr. Higginbotham is flying in first thing the next morning to accompany the body to Indianapolis. The arrangements at that end are simple and quiet but again very expensive." He paused and looked up from his notebook. "Mr. Higginbotham has paid all of the expenses ... out of his personal account."

"Interesting." I thought about that for a moment then asked, "What happens to the rest of her estate - aside from the copyrights?"

"Her lawyers are very tight-lipped about that. I'm still working on it, but, right now, I just don't know."

He read the inquisitive look on my face and added, "I've got people checking the neighborhood where the body was found. I've got a couple of men working this neighborhood. We're covering the limousine company, the hotel, the morgue, the airport. Everywhere, everything. We're rechecking every detail. We're brainstorming to find new dimensions. We're just not getting anywhere."

"I understand." And I did understand. He was asking me to suspend the investigation. He wasn't a quitter but he felt like he was wasting my money. I sent him back to work with instructions to persist. I also wanted a weekly, written report on everything.

And Scotch!

Chapter 20

Parenthood remains the greatest single preserve of the amateur.

~*Alvin Toffler*

With Scotch and water in hand, I went to my desk. I grimaced when I saw the note on my calendar. A four o'clock appointment, today. Damn! Sam had called and gave me some very sketchy details on why I had an appointment with another lawyer. I checked my watch; it was three-fifteen. I didn't even have time to brood over all that was going on. I just had to follow the paths laid out for me by those people I trusted.

Troy Lewis was an adequate attorney. He was Board Certified in divorce and custody cases. Sam had told me both of these facts when he had called this morning. I had no idea what Board Certified meant. It sounded high-powered and professional; although, it sounded very contradictory to the way Sam had said 'adequate.'

I trusted Sam. He knew the law and he knew how to win. If he wanted Lewis to handle that damned restraining order, Lewis must be the right guy.

I got to Lewis' office right at four o'clock and told his receptionist Sam Twilly had sent me. Lewis kept me waiting for 45 minutes. I finally got into his office and it was in disarray. Books, notepads, manila folders, papers, and McDonalds' bags were pell-mell on his battered desk. His office looked like the office of a shoddy private eye in a cheap detective novel. I tried to memorize the room for my next cheap detective novel. Hermon Press would love this place.

Sam knew the law. He knew lawyers and judges and he knew how to win. I trusted Sam. I decided, however, to recheck the definitions of 'trusting' and 'gullible.'

Lewis was build like a bear cub. He was about five three and weighed two hundred pounds. His salt-and-pepper hair was going mostly to salt. His clothes looked good enough for the office but I surely hoped his good suit was in the cleaners.

He dug around on his desk and found the copy of the re-straining order he'd gotten from Sam. After glancing over the order, he told me not to worry. He explained in legal terminology what it said. If I had understood what he was saying, I could have just read the document and understood *it*. When I asked him what he was saying, he smiled and translated it into English, albeit sprinkled with legal jargon.

"So the judge granted the restraining order on just her side of the story?" I asked to be sure I understood.

"Yes. It's an ex-parte order. One-sided," he translated at my grimace. "That's why there's a court date set for next Monday. The judge will hear your side of the story and decide what's best for the children."

Grudgingly, I admitted that it made a lopsided kind of sense. "Are you going to be ready by Monday?"

"I've petitioned the court to hear this case on Friday, Mr. Noble." He raised a pudgy little hand to stay my objection. After a moment's pause he told me, "Mr. Noble, I know what you see when you look at me. You see a fat little man whose suit is wearing his lunch. You're concerned that I might not be able to handle your case and you're even more concerned because I've already started changing things without talking to you first. Rest assured, Mr. Noble, I'm very capable. I've been in this business a long time and there's a very important character to civil law. Civil law is ten percent legalistics and ninety percent theatrics. I'm a very good actor and I know how to move the pieces to present the image we want the judge to see."

"This weekend coming up is the third weekend of the month. Your custody agreement says you can have your children on the first and third and fifth weekends of the month. If we don't go to court this week, we send a signal to the judge, and to your ex-wife, that missing possession of the children for one of *your* weekends is alright with you. Therefore, I moved the faulty piece so we show the judge you're concerned for your rights and for the wellbeing of the children. Theatrics.

"Do you know why Sam Twilly sent you to me?"

When I told him that I was sure Sam knew where to send me for the best counseling available, he chuckled. "Mr. Noble, I'm very good in the civil law arena, but Sam is better - much better. However, I'm Board Certified. By retaining me, you look to the judge like a guy who wants to get a specialist. That is always a valuable trait with cases involving children. It sends a subconscious message. You're subtly telling the judge that when the children need something, you'll get a specialist. Theatrics. Sam would be a little better at manipulating things in the courtroom, but he is a business or contracts lawyer. I have a pedigree.

"Chris Taravella would be much better than either of us or both of us combined. But we don't want to tip your ex-wife off that you've retained a guy whose prime function is to get you off of a murder rap. That would kill us in the custody issue." This was a simple case, he told me. "Since the police aren't filing charges against you, your ex-wife doesn't have any grounds for the restraint."

"And if they do file charges?"

"One step at a time, Mr. Noble. One step at a time." He made a lot of sense and assured me he would be ready on Friday. I still doubted he could find his way out of this hovel by then. He sounded so confident I wanted to believe. He looked so disorganized I wanted to panic. Sam said Lewis was the best man for the job on this issue. I didn't panic. I trusted Sam. I really did. I'd still recheck those definitions.

Chapter 21

The strictest justice is sometimes the greatest injustice.

~Terrence

I stopped at an all-day breakfast diner and ate on the way home. I couldn't remember when I had eaten last. I seemed to be living on coffee, Scotch, and adrenaline. I took my time and ate well. My order was simple and well cooked and I wasn't in my part of town. I had no reason to believe I'd be bothered or upset.

The quiet time in the nearly deserted diner was relaxing and I felt much better when I turned onto the freeway for the drive home. It was a typical south Texas summer evening - still light at seven-thirty when I pulled into my driveway. Light enough for me to see the man sitting on the curb in front of my house.

He was perhaps fifty and dressed in a shirt and loose tie. The late model Ford sitting on the street looked like it had been used hard and not particularly well cared for. The old cowboys would say it was rode hard and put up wet.

I had no idea who the man was or what he wanted, but he was going to have to meet me on my own terms. He stood up as I pulled up to the garage and started to walk around to meet me. I opened the garage door and went inside while this fellow was ambling around the corner of the house.

I kept a .357 magnum in the garage, in a drawer in the workbench. I kept moving inside the garage as if I hadn't seen my guest and opened the drawer. The gun was a snub-nosed revolver and I slipped it into my pocket and picked up a wrench. I turned back toward the truck.

"Howdy," called the man with the loose tie. He too had a gun in a small holster clipped to his belt.

"Can I help you with something," I asked.

He stopped at the garage door and smiled. "If you're John Noble, you can."

"If I was John Noble, how could I help you?"

Again he smiled. "You're a careful man, Mr. Noble. I like that, especially in this town. I'm Lieutenant Rod Kisselberg. I got a badge and identification papers. Garza said you'll want to call in and check me out."

"What do you want, Lieutenant?"

"I'd just like to talk to you for a few minutes. About murder, Army days, and such things. It's not official and I got no warrant."

I did take his identification and call him in to SAPD. He checked out so I let him in. I wasn't going to get any work done tonight or get back on my schedule, so I figured I might as well find out what the coppers knew.

We went inside. Actually, I let him in the front door. I had locked the garage when I came in to call SAPD. "What do you want to talk about, Lieutenant?"

"Let me tell you, Mr. Noble, the case against you is airtight. He was speaking patiently and deliberately. He had just been assigned to Diana's case.

"It's not too airtight, Lieutenant, because I'm innocent." Before he could tell me I was being naive, I continued, "Since I didn't commit the crime, there's got to be a flaw in the evidence somewhere. *And* it's your job to find it!"

He smiled at me and asked, "Aren't you going to tell me that innocent has to count for something?"

"I'm not a child!" I snapped. "Nor am I finding this whole affair, or your visit, as entertaining as you seem to be."

"Mr. Noble, I understand your anxiety, but I came here tonight to relieve you some. I'm not here to arrest you. As a matter of fact, I'm off duty for the next three weeks."

"Great! Diana's case goes on hold while you're taking a break? What came up, Lieutenant, an important fishing trip?" I was furious. This mess would drag out long enough if everybody who was working on it, was working on it.

"On the contrary, Mr. Noble. I'll be fishing but not like you mean. I've got a cold six pack in the car; mind if I get it? You and I need to talk and I talk best with a beer in my hand."

He had already gotten up and started for the door. I didn't really want to drink beer with a fellow I was sure was going to arrest me. I started to object to the beer when the phone rang.

"I'll give you some privacy while you take your call," he said over his shoulder and went outside.

Damn! Diana had been dead less than a week, I'm the prime suspect, and I'm starting to lose my composure. I lit a cigarette and grabbed the phone.

"Mr. Noble, this is Kathleen Homan. I'm sorry, Mr. Noble, but with all that's going on, I'm afraid the boys can't do your yard work any longer."

"Kathy, what are you talking about?"

She always called me Mr. Noble but now it sounded like an accusation. "Mr. Noble, I know you didn't kill that poor girl, but with the way people talk, and the police at your house, and everything else ..." She sort of faded out and then found her courage again. "I just don't think it's good for Todd and Ted to be around you. I'm sorry."

"Kathy, those boys have been cutting my grass and doing odd jobs for me for five years. Now suddenly they don't want to come back. I find that hard to believe!"

"Mr. Noble, I know you've been very kind to my boys. Ever since their father died, you've done a lot for them. I know you've more than overpaid them for the work they do and I appreciate it. But, I'm their mother and I have to do what I think is best for them. And I think it's best if they stay away from you. They're good boys, Mr. Noble. Please understand."

She was strained and I could tell she had been through the same argument with the boys. "Mrs. Homan, I'm tired of being patient and being told to 'please understand' about everybody shunning me. I want you to understand! You're right they are good boys - like their father. You've forced this idea on them and they didn't like it. Like their father, they don't want to turn their backs on a friend." I was mad and didn't care who knew it.

"Please understand, Mr. Noble." She hung up.

I'd been too hard on her and I knew it but at the moment I just didn't care.

Kisselberg came back in with a small cooler. He brought out a beer and offered it to me. "You need something to cool your phone slamming hand."

"Damn you, Kisselberg. I don't need your brand of humor or your damned beer! You came here with something to say. Say it and get out!"

He took his time opening the beer, took a sip and then looked at me out of the hardest eyes I've ever seen. "Sergeant Garza has been appointed to a special task force. Your case is considered closed and you were to be arrested this morning."

"So why wasn't I?" I was still mad yet the thought of being arrested cooled me off some.

"I got the Captain to give me some time to snoop around - off duty!" He took a long drink from his beer.

Well, that surprised me a little. That is the kind of thing really good TV cops might do. Kisselberg didn't strike me as a really good TV cop. He looked and acted like a combination of Colombo and Wyatt Earp.

"I'm not going to look a gift horse in the mouth, Lieutenant," I said as I pulled one of his beers out of the cooler. "But, why?"

"You're innocent." He opened his second beer.

I was a little more than surprised at his statement. As he explained, I almost felt like a minor character in one of my own stories.

He said the case SAPD had was airtight. I had a motive - the mutual death clause in my contract with the victim. I argued that there was much more money to be made by writing new books with Hoyle's characters. He countered that argument with, "There still is." He reminded me of the royalties I inherited from Diana. Of course, he was right. Most of Hoyle's books were still selling and I now owned all of the copyrights outright.

I certainly had the opportunity. Diana was here 'til two in the afternoon the day before she was killed. The public fight we had two days earlier was known. Her clothes were found in my truck - in my garage.

"I've explained all those things; I mean the ones I could. Some of the things are a mystery to me."

He smiled, "There are three ways I can look at this. One way is that you murdered Mrs. Faire and you're so stupid you left a trail a blind man could follow. Another way is that you killed the girl and you're so smart you stacked the evidence against yourself so heavily that it would look like a frame and you'd get off." He paused and looked at me.

"The last way to look at this mess is that someone else killed her and is framing you for murder." After another pause, he asked, "Where's your bathroom?"

When he came back, he opened his next beer and bummed a cigarette. I hadn't smoked in four years but a murder charge is unsettling, to say the least. I've known ex-smokers who said the urge was still there twenty years later and major events could start you off again. Damn!

"Alright, Lieutenant, you said I am innocent so I take it you think I'm being framed. Tell me why you think so."

"Well, part of it is cop intuition." He could see from my expression that I wasn't a fan of intuition. "Instinct is just a collection of memories you've forgotten that come back to haunt you," he told me. "You're a man of words, Mr. Noble, not feelings. So, let me put my instinct into English. First, I've read some of your work. You put too much thought into your work to be stupid. That rules out the first option. Second, no matter what some of my colleagues say, you're also not smart enough to set up all of the evidence to point at you. You can do that on paper but not in life.

"Besides, some of the marks against you are years old. I can't believe you've planned this crime so perfectly that you drew Mrs. Faire to you to write her father's unfinished stories. You're good but not that good."

"What do you mean about old evidence?"

"Army Special Forces for eighteen months. Discharged with a General Discharge under Honorable conditions. You got that changed to an Honorable Discharge six months later, but the records are there if you know where to look."

"So I got kicked out of the Army. That doesn't have anything to do with this." I didn't see any connection.

"The two incidents didn't seem to be related until I read your Army records. The Army said officially you weren't suited for service. The fact that they couldn't prove aggravated assault charges against you is the real reason they let you go. That and your Special Forces training go against you."

"You've got a history of violence and enough martial arts training to kill with your hands." The Lieutenant had also talked to some Army people who were willing to discuss things that weren't on the record.

Kisselberg also mentioned an incident from about three years ago. It was right before my divorce. Harriet had accused me of wholesale infidelity. I ran into her one evening in a restaurant. She was dining with some guy about thirty years old. Kind of a handsome fellow, I guess. I'd been having a lot of frustration with my work and I was mad - and drunk. When I saw them together, I started yelling and grabbed the guy. He was a tough, capable man and after I got the fight started, I had to really hurt him to keep him down. It turned out he was her private investigator.

Sam Twilly did some magic and kept me out of jail. He even got the charges dropped but that little indiscretion cost me custody of the kids. I figured that was the end of the incident. Now it could get me convicted of murder.

He put out his cigarette and said, "There's enough pieces of evidence that you couldn't have stacked against yourself - things that happened before you even met Diana Faire. So you're not slick enough to have framed yourself."

He started to pick up his empty beer cans and added, "You're certainly not stupid enough to throw her clothes in the back of your truck and leave them there." He stuck the cans in his cooler and got ready to leave.

"So you think I'm being framed?"

"No. I don't actually think that, but it's the only option that I can't logically rule out, using intuition.

"There's two more things. I'm trying to prove you're innocent." He paused and stared at me, "There's at least two private investigators working on this case and I'll be surprised if there isn't four or five. Some company in Wisconsin hired a PI who used to be my partner. He told me there's another one who's working for some folks out west."

"From what you've told me about Higginbotham, he's probably put somebody on the street. The way I hear it on the grapevine, all of the unofficial police are out to salt you away."

"You said two things, Lieutenant." I reminded him.

"Oh, yeah. Don't leave town." He chuckled and told me I could use that in my next book.

The 'folks out west' were surely Diana's sisters. After all, if I got convicted, they would have legal grounds to get the contract revoked. Kisselberg believed they were prime suspects in the murder. I didn't know what to think about their involvement, except that Diana was frightened of them. It would make more sense, on their part, to kill me first and then Diana. But from all I'd heard and seen, common sense didn't abound in that family. Of course, if they did have a contract out on her, they just might not have had time to call off their hit man.

Kisselberg also suspected Higginbotham may have killed Diana. That was unbelievable. The lieutenant could suspect all he wanted, but I had seen Higginbotham. He was gallant in her defense, and awed in her presence, and ate up with the worst case of puppy love imaginable. I could accept the idea of the old lawyer being furious at being left out of the contract signing. He may have tried to kill me but never Diana. He would have died for her. And he would have certainly set some bloodhounds on the trail of her murderer. Kisselberg said he confirmed that Higginbotham was on the flight to Indianapolis hours before Diana's death.

It was late enough to start working but I just wasn't up to it after the day I'd had.

Chapter 22

When we remember that we are all mad, the mysteries disappear and life stands explained.

~Mark Twain

I had only slept a couple of hours. I was tired but too keyed up to rest. What little sleep I'd gotten had been full of restless dreams. Murders, cops, lawyers, and monsters attacked me in dreamland and fighting them off had left me more exhausted than I was before I had laid down. I paced the house and tried to focus on something tangible. Work wasn't the answer because even awake my thoughts were as wispy as dream thoughts. I did odd chores and housework. Any brainless task that came into my disheveled thinking got my full attention. As full as it was!

At five o'clock, or there about, I fell into a blissful, dreamless slumber. At noon I got up, showered, and ate.

Routine. A work schedule. My schedule. These were the things I needed to pull me back together. I went through the mundane, usually hated, business tasks. I found a childish pleasure in doing the things I most disliked doing. It was my life and I was back in control of it! Diana wasn't there when I read the fan mail. Kisselberg was nowhere to be found when I was paying the bills! All of the lawyers were in hiding when I hunted through my files for the information on Colorado!

There was a measure of glee in just being left alone with boring tasks. Was I cracking up? Was this whole mess driving me nuts? I needed a 'sanity check' as we had called it in the Army. I had to talk to someone outside of the immediate problem. I needed to touch reality and be sure it was still there.

I knew who to call.

"Stonemason Literary Agency. May I help you?" Mrs. Cooper said into the phone.

"Hello, Mrs. Cooper. I received a thank you card from you for the flowers I sent. Your thanks wasn't needed. How have you been, dear lady?"

"Hello, Mr. Noble. I'm glad you called. Mr. Stonemason wanted to talk to you and instructed me to call, but not too early. Just a moment and I'll get him on the line for you." Mrs. Cooper understood my unorthodox schedule and Chucky knew not to call me in the morning.

"No, Mrs. Cooper. I didn't call to talk to Chucky. I wanted to speak with you for a moment." She really was a sweet old lady and I liked talking to her. Chucky would want to talk business and he was part of the mess I wanted to put aside for a while.

"Well, Mr. Noble, I don't know if I can help you or not, but I'll certainly try." She was a little confused. Chucky always talked to the clients and she didn't know what sort of business I wanted.

"It's not business, Mrs. Cooper. In fact, I just wanted to talk to a friendly face. You're a sweet lady and I don't spend enough time remembering the really good people I know." I hoped she wouldn't think I was making a pass at her. She probably thought I was drunk but hesitant or not she was the kind of person I really needed to chat with at the moment.

We chit-chatted for half an hour and I felt good - great. There were real people out there! I could tell I was interrupting her work and she was wanting to get back to it. "Well, Mrs.

Cooper, it's been great talking to you. Like I said, I just sort of needed a friendly face. Thanks."

"Yes, Mr. Noble, it was nice talking to you, too. But before you go, Mr. Stonemason really did want to speak to you. If you'll let me get him now, then I know I won't have to worry about waking you when I call." She really was a nice lady.

"Well, I suppose I can spare a few moments for good ole Chucky." She put me on hold and the telephone started serenading me with elevator music.

"Good afternoon, John. How's Texas?" Chucky sounded more jovial than usual. And the happy mood sounded forced.

"Texas is wonderful, Chucky, just like it was when you were here. What kind of business have you got for me?" Chucky was a tremendous agent and made my career boom when it could easily have busted. Even though I'd seen Chucky so smoothly wrap Diana and others around his finger, I could always tell when he was buttering me up. That usually meant he had a job for me that I wouldn't particularly want.

"Three magazine articles, John." He abandoned the soft soap and got right down to business. "They are to be historical pieces about authentic old west sites. This is a great opportunity to get your Western by-line back in the publisher's mind. That will help when your next Western comes out." He went on to recite some specifics about the assignment and the payment. He ended by extolling the benefits to my career.

"Chucky, you've lost it. First of all, I've sworn off magazine articles and you know it. You also know I decided to quit doing them because they interfere with the work I love doing. Furthermore, even if I wanted to do them, I couldn't. I'd have to go to Utah and Nevada to do research. The coppers won't let me leave town, much less Texas." I explained all of my reasons more for my benefit than for Chucky's. I hadn't really examined the limitations on my life and now that I had, I didn't like them.

"Chucky, I'd say you're really slipping but I don't think you are. What's the real reason for this call?"

He cleared his throat. "John, you know me too well. I've got something to tell you that's probably going to make you mad."

I almost laughed at that. In the last two weeks, I'd been bombarded with annoying people, I'd been unable to work, I'd lost my kids, had a friend killed, and been accused of murder. I didn't have any anger left to give. "I'll try not to yell, Chucky."

"Well, you can bet I yelled plenty when I got this news. *The Press Papers* isn't going to print for a while." He said it kind of quickly like it wouldn't hurt so bad if it was fast.

The Press Papers was my third Hermon Press novel. The publisher had just bought it less than a month ago. It made no sense for them not to print the book. True to my promise I didn't yell. "Why not?"

"They're beating their lips about their work schedules and cash flow. The truth, John, is all of the excuses they gave me are flimsy at best. I called one of the senior editors and did some pleading. He finally admitted they are holding the manuscript because of the murder. They're afraid of some bad publicity."

Chucky talked for another fifteen minutes explaining all he had been able to coerce out of the publisher's top people. I finally got tired of listening.

"Chucky, call them back and tell them to go to print or go to Hell! If they don't do it now, the deal's off. Period!" I still wasn't yelling, but I was mad. Here again, I was getting treated like a mad-dog criminal without the benefit of a trial. I was really mad!

"It's not quite that simple. I've reviewed the contract and my legal staff has gone over it. They've got us by a loophole, John. They aren't violating the agreement unless they refuse to print at all. This is a tough one, John."

"Chucky, I said I wasn't going to yell, so I'm not. Here's the deal from my end of it. They are refusing to honor our deal because I might be a murderer. Therefore they are violating my civil rights. I'm a well-established author and we can get published in another house. Cancel the deal!"

"Now, John ... "

"Cancel the deal!" I was close to yelling.

"John, I'm not sure if we can ..." Chucky was hesitant because he didn't want to make me any madder than I already was.

"I'm sure! Chucky there's someone at my door. I'll talk to you next week. Goodbye." He could handle the manipulations of business as long as he knew I was serious about what I wanted. And I was dead serious.

Someone seriously wanted me to answer the door. It wasn't irritating just persistent. Maybe irritating only came when persistent interrupts your sleep. Who knows?

"Are you John Noble?" They asked when I answered the door. Seems everyone was pounding on my door to ask me if I'm me. But, at least, these two ladies were the only ones in the last two weeks to show up here at a decent hour. I told them who I was after complimenting them on their timing. They seemed confused by the compliment, so I asked them what they wanted.

They were dressed too well to be welcome-wagon ladies or to be collecting for some worthy cause. There was no car in sight but they hadn't been in the sun very long. The outward appearances of the ladies were pretty ordinary. They were both in their early forties and there was nothing uncommon about them.

Nothing, that is, except their escorts. The two men standing behind them looked like 1930's shoulder strikers in modern dress. Not that these guys were old, early thirties probably, they just looked out of place with the two ladies. These guys would have looked right at home behind Al Capone or Frank Nitti. One of them, at least, was armed. Although his suit was tailored to hide the shoulder holster, it wasn't doing a complete job.

My .41 magnum was in my waistband, in the small of my back.

The taller of the ladies asked if they could come in. "We have a matter to discuss with you." She was polite but not friendly.

"No," I said flatly. They weren't ready for refusal. In fact, the other lady had already started to step forward. As their surprise turned to irritation, I added, "I'm not in the habit of inviting unidentified, armed people into my home."

The taller lady, also older I believed, recovered quickly. "Armed? Come now, Mr. Noble." She tried to be clever and reassuring all at once. She spoke with the air of a parent speaking to a misbehaving, over-imaginative child.

I wasn't buying it. I put my left hand on the door frame and my right, loosely folded, on my hip at belt height.

"Surely, you don't mean to make us stand in this heat, Mr. Noble." She was still using that mildly scolding tone. I just stared into her eyes.

"Come on, Sarah." The younger lady put her hand on the other's arm and turned to leave. The shoulder strikers stepped dutifully out of the way.

These women were, I was sure, Drucilla and Lucinda, the evil step-sisters. No wonder Diana had feared them!

I called Matt Brown and gave him their names and descriptions. I also described the two shoulder strikers. I would see them all again, I was sure. There was no reason for them to be in San Antonio except to see me. I wanted to know everything they did and everywhere they went. I also asked Matt to get all of the background data on them that he could.

Matt had made the comment earlier that this murder was going to solve the unemployment problem in San Antonio. He was being facetious, but ... this was getting more and more snarled.

Chapter 23

Whatever limits us we call Fate.

~Ralph Waldo Emerson

After I had hung up with Matt, I started to call Sam at his home. I usually didn't call him there because he considered it his haven; however, I was past the point of usual. Everything seemed to be cascading down on me in quick order.

I hung up the phone before it even rang. I remembered that Sam was in Indianapolis. They were probating Diana's will the next morning and he went to represent me at the proceedings.

Since I couldn't talk to him, I went to my desk and wrote him a short note. I told him about the publishers pulling my book and the visit from Diana's sisters. My fax machine seemed to take forever to warm up, so I went to the bar and poured myself some Scotch. After sending the message to Sam's office, I sent another empty Scotch bottle to the trash can.

I woke up on top of the bed again. Well, I was saving a lot of time making the bed. And, the way my head felt, I didn't want to try any tedious tasks. The sun was bright enough to trim my heavy drapes with lemon light. It was about nine in the morning and I grumbled all the way to the kitchen. My schedule was shot and I couldn't even recall what, if anything, I was working on.

The rest of the day was fairly blurry. Work, or an attempt at such, household chores, and boredom blended into one another to form a memoryless day. There was one high point, at least one that I can recall. Beth and Sarah returned late in the afternoon.

They had called first and asked for an interview. I told them to come at four o'clock. Then I called Matt and told him to be here at half past three. He brought two rather rugged looking men with him. Matt told me that his associates were along to ensure the interview didn't get rough. From the looks of them, I was afraid if it didn't get rough, they would be disappointed. But, I was glad they were there.

What strange turns life takes. Two weeks ago all I was concerned about was someone beating on my door at an uncouth hour. Now I was worried about uncouth people beating in my head. Meade and Culpetzer, Matt's men, were typical bodyguard types. Both looked very capable in a street fight and both were armed. I knew Matt was carrying his 9mm automatic. I had my .41 and then wondered what I really expected to happen. A hundred years ago this kind of precaution would have been commonplace ... but now? I felt a little silly, yet scared, too. I felt like one of the Earp boys heading for the OK Corral. This was crazy, but those women were for real and I had felt Diana's fears when I first met them. Silly or not, caution cost so little.

They were a half hour late; I guess it was supposed to make me more nervous. Maybe they just weren't punctual people, but I had to suspect the worst from them.

I let them into the dining room and asked what they wanted. They said they were sure I had killed their "baby sister" to get possession of their father's copyrights. The general attitude that these two displayed was almost convincing. They seemed frank and to the point, and wanted me to know I'd never profit by my crime. The only thing out of place in their attitude was that they didn't seem in the least bereft. They were discussing business - just business - but using terms of endearment for Diana.

I told them I suspected they had killed her and threw them out. Sarah, definitely the older of the two, got a bit indignant but Beth kept her under control. It often seems to be the case with siblings: the elder one is dynamic and forceful while the younger one is the peacemaker. That's how these sisters were.

Matt was a little disappointed. Beth and Sarah had been wearing gloves like they had come to a fancy tea or something. Their bodyguards had touched nothing. Matt said he really wanted to get some fingerprints. I guess it just wasn't meant to be.

I spent a fitful night. I was angry at having to be in court so early the next morning. Early or not, I was there on time and so was Troy Lewis.

He met me in the hall and was bright and upbeat. He had obviously gotten his good suit out of the cleaners. He spent a few minutes preparing me for what was to come and offering me confidence. The hearing was exactly like he had said it would be. The judge heard both sides of the issue and decided Harriet had no grounds for a restraining order. The order was revoked and we all went our separate ways. I did notice that Beth and Sarah were in the audience for the hearing. The rest of the day was a bit blurry; I didn't drink because I had to pick up the kids in the evening, but I don't recall what I did.

Harriet was cold and very formal when I picked up the twins. She didn't say anything about court or much of anything else. She was obviously very mad but I just didn't care. In fact, it was the first time in a year I had been in her house without feeling queasy. I liked the feeling and thought maybe I was getting stronger.

The weekend started just like all of the others: pizza, movie rentals, general goofing around, and home for video games and horror movies. The kids fell asleep on the movies again.

Saturday and Sunday buzzed by without anything to mar the tranquility of weekend parenting. The kids enjoyed themselves, and I enjoyed them.

I'll probably always look back on that weekend as one of the high points of my life.

My children were people, or at least, they would grow up to be people. However, they were the only people I didn't want to be excluded from my life. People complicate life, but these two people brought a delightful complication. I loved our time together!

Chapter 24

Love demands infinitely less than friendship.

~George Jean Nathan

"Mr. Noble," the voice on the phone began. It was an almost timid mixture of question and statement. She continued in that half-apologetic, half-probing manner, "I'm aware, sir, that you've been beset by people and problems surrounding the murder of your friend, Diana Faire."

"What do you want, lady?" I snapped.

In the same patient, yet determined voice, she said, "I was told to say 'One second to look at that paper or a lifetime of regret. The choice is yours, John.'" There was a pause. "Miss Faire said you'd remember that phrase. She said if she died and I needed to talk to you, that phrase would serve as my credentials."

After another pause, "If I've brought a painful memory, I hope that I can make amends to both you and to Miss Faire's name."

Another damned mystery. She quoted some words that passed between Diana and me, alone. Diana had to have told her - and done so for a reason. She, the strange voice on the phone, could be a link to the past. Maybe she could provide the missing piece to the puzzle. What was it Kisselberg had called it? 'The fly in the ointment.'

Carefully, I asked, "If I accept your credentials, what do you want from me?"

"A small chat, sir."

"Why?"

"I'd prefer not to discuss it on the phone, sir."

My interest was high. This was someone I wanted to talk to. But she was right, not on the phone. Not here either; there had been too many people in my house lately. I asked where she was and agreed to meet her at her motel. Then I called Matt and told him to check my house and phones for bugs.

The motel was one of those traveler's inns that went cheap. It didn't even have a restaurant. It wasn't one of those flea-bag dives on the poor side of town, just a low-expense, moderately clean motel. She had told me she was in Room 142.

There was a late model Chevy in the parking space marked for her room. It had Indiana plates and an Indianapolis Colts bumper sticker. The car was dirty and dented a little and had a U-Haul car-top carrier strapped on it.

I parked in one of the unnumbered slots along the fence. I sat in the truck for a few minutes studying the car and the door with the white numerals one-four-two on it.

I didn't know what more I was getting in to. So little time had passed since Diana woke me up that first morning. So many strange and interruptive events had forced themselves into my life. And now I was meeting an unknown woman in a low-rent motel because she knew some words Diana had said. I was pretty sure this woman also knew the phrase she repeated was the one Diana had used as her own, Diana's own, credentials.

Could Beth and Sarah, those denizens from Arizona be setting me up? If I died, the copyrights would be a controversial issue. Those women wanted Diana dead! So now they must want me dead.

The first time, they had showed up at my house had been unannounced and they brought two armed thugs. Would they have dared execute me in my own home in broad daylight? Last Thursday, Matt and his thugs were there to balance the forces.

How much power did these women wield and how far were they willing to go? I had to push Matt to get me the info on them. They had ransacked Diana's home - or so I had been told. Were they untouchable? Diana had money; she could have struck back at them outside legal channels. Had she? What kind of people was I dealing with?

Could the mystery woman in 142 be bait for a trap? She knew the words Diana had spoken to me in my home. Her credentials were good. She wasn't in with the half-sisters. She had to be an ally of Diana's. Did that make her an ally of mine? I couldn't say. What was the old question? 'Is the enemy of my enemy my friend, or not?' She may not be on my side, but I felt sure she was somewhat safe.

Somewhat!

I checked my pistol. Sure of its condition, I slipped it into my waistband under my sports coat. For a little extra protection, I went to the manager's office. The sleepy clerk left his TV movie reluctantly and answered questions even more reluctantly. For twenty bucks he gave me the name and address of the lady in 142.

She was registered as Noel Caine with a Fishers, Indiana address. Where the heck was Fishers Indiana? The name matched the one she'd given on the phone. That didn't mean much, but it was something.

I used the payphone. Matt answered his phone on the second ring. I gave him all of the information I'd bought from the motel's night manager. I also gave him the license number for the car in front of Ms. Caine's door. Matt offered to come over and loiter in the parking lot. I told him I'd be fine and thanked him for his concern. I didn't want to scare this woman off with a posse. Matt knew all he would need to know if something happened here.

Nothing was going to happen. I was sure. I had enough protection. My knock on door number 142 brought a question.

"This is John Noble, Ms. Caine." I think that was the first time I'd spoken my name in weeks when it wasn't in response to someone hammering on *my* door. It felt good to change things around.

A short, stocky redhead opened the door and asked me in. She had a turned-up nose with a field of freckles across it. Her mouth was rather full and she had very green eyes. Her face was pleasant, not pretty. "Please come in, sir."

The room was standard for the type of motel. There was a double bed in the corner covered with a nondescript bedspread. The only nightstand was mounted into the wall as was the double chest of drawers. A small, round table, complete with two armchairs, was pushed against the groaning air conditioner under the window. The heavy drapes, matching the bedspread, were closed. There were wall-mounted lamps and a mirror.

Noel Caine stepped into the middle of the room with her hands hanging at her sides. She had walked with her back to me, then turned around. She was wearing a thin, white cotton blouse tucked into a beige skirt. Her shoes were beside the bed and she stood there in her hose. She presented a very non-threatening image.

"My ID is on the table, Mr. Noble. I'm sure you want to see it."

I still stood in the doorway. I was taking in all I could see and listening for any sound from outside. "Why should I?"

"Your dealings with my employer have placed you in danger. Miss Faire said you were very cautious. I'm just trying to make it easier for you, sir."

She was making it easy. Why? I stepped into the room and glanced at the papers on the table. An Indiana driver's license, a private investigator's license and a permit to carry a concealed weapon were spread out in a neat row by her purse.

I touched each document as I read it. When my fingers rested on the gun permit, she said, "The weapon is a snub-nosed .38 in my purse. If you're satisfied, sir, I suggest we close the door."

"Who hired you, Noel?"

"Diana Faire. Before she died. The door, please?"

I picked up her purse then walked into the bathroom. It was empty. She hadn't moved, only her eyes followed me. "Yes," I said, "let's close the door." I dropped her purse on the bed.

"You're private heat from Indiana and you say Miss Faire hired you. Why should I believe you?"

"Mr. Noble, if you'd care to sit down, I'll tell you all about me and why I'm here." Her eyes had a pleading look.

I had wanted her story; that's why I came here. When I sat at the table, I chose the chair near the now-closed door. She sat opposite me and scooped up her papers with trembling hands. I wondered at her pleading eyes, timid voice, and shaking hands. If she was a private investigator, she was the most frightened one I'd ever met. I planned to keep her off balance.

"If Miss Faire hired you," I started to speak just as she did. "If Miss Faire hired you, you must know her death ended your employment. There's not going to be any more money. What's your angle?"

"Money's not an object, Mr. Noble. Not in this case." She said it like she meant it, really meant it. In light of her surroundings and transportation, it didn't have the same effect when she said it as when Diana said it or even if I had said it. She paused momentarily, took a deep breath, and looked me in the eye. "First of all, Diana has been using my services for a long time. She left an envelope in my safe to be opened in the event of her death. Her murder is really what she meant and we both knew it. The envelope contained a two-year retainer and instructions to find her killer.

It took a couple of hours for her to tell her story. She and Diana had gone to college together and had been friends for years. Noel had been the one who tracked me down for Diana. She was also the one Diana had hired to keep track of Beth and Sarah. Noel Caine had investigated the burglary and vandalism in Diana's house and tried to track down the hate mail that kept coming to her friend.

This woman knew a lot about Diana's sisters and openly hated them. She said she had complete dossiers on both of them and on most of their hired thugs. "They are criminal and unscrupulous women who would stop at nothing." The anger and bitterness in her voice were unprofessional. I said so.

She seemed a little surprised at my bluntness. "I told you, Mr. Noble, that money was no object. This is a personal case for me. Very personal! You see, Diana and I were lovers."

Well, that shocked me. For a moment I was speechless. She'd been looking me right in the eye when she said it. She was serious.

This was definitely a new piece of the puzzle but not one that promised to help me. I said lamely, "Diana was married."

Her eyes were still on my face and there was a tear on her cheek. She studied me for a long moment to decide if I was one of those people who thought someone couldn't possibly be both gay and married. She rightly decided I didn't believe that nonsense. "Her marriage failed because her husband didn't measure up to her father. She had a couple of other relationships that failed for the same reason."

"We were very different, Mr. Noble. I'm a lesbian. I'm not a man hater; I just don't like men sexually. Diana liked men. Loved men. But subconsciously she compared every man in her life to Mr. Hoyle. They all left her disappointed. Our relationship developed out of mutual needs."

She wiped the tears from her face. "I love her, Mr. Noble. I really do. I'm going to find her killer because he hurt me."

She went to the bathroom and left me feeling very uncomfortable. She returned with red eyes but seemed composed.

"Mr. Noble ..."

"Call me John." Then I added, "But not Johnny."

She smiled, "I know. You hate Johnny. Diana told me."

"I'd like a drink before we continue our talk. Do you feel up to going out for one?" I could see she needed a drink. I needed one badly.

"I'm hungry, John. Diana and I have never told anyone about our relationship. I told you because I'm going to need your help in solving this murder. You didn't kill my Diana. Her evil sisters didn't do it. I'm a little lost; that's why I came to see you. I told you about us so you'd understand why I'm here. But you know something? I feel so much better now that I've talked to someone about Diana. Thanks for listening."

I wondered if she'd still feel like thanking me when I told her I'd slept with her lover. I had to tell her. I don't know exactly why but I felt like I had to tell her.

After a drink!

We went to a little French restaurant that had secluded booths and soft music. Not soft music that was romantic but the kind you could talk over easily. I liked the booths so Noel could cry or cuss at me with some privacy and dignity. The biggest attraction in the restaurant was that they served my brand of Scotch as well as dinner.

After we had ordered our food and I was waiting for my second double Scotch to come, I told her that Diana and I had made love.

She smiled and I think it was at my nervousness. "I know. Diana told me. Don't worry; I'm not angry."

"Jealous?"

"No. Yes. I don't know. I'm not jealous of your lovemaking. I told you Diana and I were different. I don't like lima beans but I don't care if others eat them. Even Diana. She loved men, but none of them were good enough for her standards. I may be jealous because you might have been the right man for her. I don't know, John. I just don't know."

Our food came and she ate with a passion. I nursed my third drink. If Noel thought Diana might have left her for me, she could be the killer. I'd read somewhere that love was a much more common motive for murder than was money.

After the meal, we talked about the case. She explained that she was sure from the things Diana had said about me that I wasn't the killer. She had said earlier the half-sisters weren't guilty and I asked why she thought so.

"I know those two, John. They don't want the copyrights. They don't even want the money. They just wanted to make Diana suffer and then die. They are that cruel. She had called them and told them about your contract. They knew you'd inherit. So killing her then would not have been enough. They had to make her suffer. They would have had you killed and then Diana would have been right back where she was a month ago."

I asked about some hitman not knowing about the contract. My old theory that the sisters may have sent someone out and couldn't pull him back in time. Noel didn't seem to buy it. She said the sisters kept too tight a grip on all that was going on.

"Well, if there's no longer any torture value, Beth and Sarah have no reason to kill me, right?" I asked.

"You must try to understand the latent cruelty in those two. You foiled their plans; that's reason enough to kill you in their minds." She was serious and not speaking as someone recently bereaved.

"The police lieutenant thinks Higginbotham might have killed her. I disagree. He was madly in love with her and I just can't picture him ever hurting her."

She agreed with me and we went on through the short list of suspects. Nobody on the list seemed to have all of the ingredients needed to do the killing. Some essential element of the ideal murder was missing in each case. I didn't mention that she might be on my list of possible killers. That little bit of opinion was going to be between me and Matt Brown.

"Oh, by the way," I warned her, "Drucilla and Lucinda are in town. Be careful."

She looked puzzled. "Drucilla and Lucinda?"

"Dru and Lu are the evil step-sisters in Cinderella. Diana's life seemed to be a mixture of parts from different fairy tales and

I've adapted some of the names. Her half-sisters are in San Antonio."

She understood but I could see it bothered her to have her lover's life referred to in Cinderella terms. She finally said, "Good people don't get killed in the fairy tales."

It was past midnight when I returned home. My work schedule was ruined. I should be ready for work and all I was ready for was eight hours of sleep.

Chapter 25

Patience and the passage of time do more than strength and fury.

~*Jean de la Fontaine*

There was over a week with no interruptions. No one called to harass me; no one hammered on my door at obscene hours; no armed showdowns in my home.

Paradise Found!

Wednesday afternoons had been set aside as Taravella's time. Sam and I were there for a fact-by-fact review of the case. This afternoon Troy had joined us because Chris wanted some particulars on the custody issue. The three-hour session was grueling, demanding - so was Taravella.

As tough as the legal strategy meeting had been, the traffic at rush hour was tougher. I left the freeway for the relatively deserted city streets. There were still a lot of cars but, at least, they were moving.

I saw the supermarket sign and remembered I needed a few things. Across from the supermarket was one of my favorite signs - an all-day breakfast shop. They offered an endless supply of coffee which would do well to wash down the strategy and they would be slow enough to dilute the traffic. And, I was hungry.

Notepad in hand, I ordered coffee and eggs. Breakfast was pretty good. The waitress was cute and friendly. Writing stunk. After an hour, I'd written only a grocery list, and even it wasn't very good.

After a final smile from the waitress, I crossed the street with my twenty-item list. It was another hour and two hundred dollars later when the high-school boy with the scrawny neck put my groceries in the back of the truck. Twenty items? I had that many plastic bags full of stuff. I thought impulse grocery buying only happened when you were hungry. Oh, well, I needed the groceries.

Kisselberg was sitting on his Coleman cooler in my driveway. He was drinking a beer and there were three empty cans in front of him on the driveway. He was using one of the empty cans as an ashtray. It smoldered and smelled - obviously too full.

Paradise Lost!

"Care for a beer, Mr. Noble?" he wondered as I got out of the truck.

"No, thanks, Lieutenant. What fair wind blew you my way?" I sounded a lot more chipper than I felt.

"I just came by for a friendly chat. I'd rather chat indoors."

"I've got to get these groceries inside. Give me a hand and we can talk as we work."

He mumbled something under his breath, set his beer can on the cooler, and grabbed a double handful of plastic bags. It took us three trips to get everything in on the counter. "Canned stuff goes in that pantry over there," I told him as I started loading the refrigerator.

"In a minute." He was headed back to rescue his abandoned beer. He came back with his little cooler and his beer. Once back in the kitchen, he worked steadily.

I thanked him for his help and we sat down at the kitchen table. He offered me a beer. It was his last and he looked like he was afraid I might accept.

"No thanks. I'll have a soft drink." I got one I'd just put in the refrigerator. "What do we have to chat about, Kisselberg?"

"Have you been reading the papers, John?"

I thought he was being a bit too familiar, but there was something about this old cowboy that I liked. He and I could be friends, I thought. Except for this murder investigation. "No. Are they still writing stories about me?"

He smiled with true humor. "Not too many, I guess. But I was wondering if you've read about the "Graffiti Task Force" the mayor has started.

"Cops downtown scraping bad words off public walls. Or something like that." I'd read something about it, however, I couldn't recall the specifics.

"Something like that," he agreed. "That's where Garza went and next Monday a lot more cops are going down there to help out. Gotta clean things up for the tourists. Orders from headquarters."

"It's a pitiful system we have when we drop the real work for crap like that." I didn't know how he felt about the Task Force but I had an idea he agreed with me.

"And we were short handed before all of this started." He sat sullenly for a time, drinking his beer.

Suddenly, he said, "My vacation has been curtailed. I've got to go back to work Monday morning. The first thing I have to do when I get there is come out here and arrest you. The charge will be murder."

There was a dense silence following his announcement. My stomach churned and I hoped he couldn't hear it. He was drawing designs with the tip of his cigarette in the ashes on the bottom of the large glass ashtray.

"John. The captain would have my badge if he knew I told you." His pensive, gloomy face split with a grin. He looked up and added, "The chief would have my ass. But, I don't use it for much anymore. So, what the hell?"

"You're telling me not to skip town or spill the beans"

"Yeah." Gloom returned. "I sure hope you're here Monday when I come." As a subtle afterthought, "I hope your lawyer is, too."

I checked my watch. Eight thirty - too late to call tonight. But there was plenty of time. Tomorrow.

Kisselberg and I talked till ten. Not about the case, not about anything at all. Just talked.

"See you Monday, John." He waved and carried his cooler, full of empty cans, to his car.

His friendly manner reminded me of one of those silly cartoons where the whistle blows and the wolf and the sheepdog stop chasing each other, punch their time cards, and exchange goodnights.

Kisselberg and I were "off the clock". When the whistle blew and we clocked in, he would come to arrest me for murder. But for now, I wished him a good evening.

He was a good man.

* * *

At ten o'clock on Monday morning, Sam and I were sharing a pot of coffee. He was at my dining room table working on some things he had brought along. I was busy with household and business chores. I hated the work I was doing, but I hated the waiting even worse.

"They can't catch criminals. They can't protect our homes and neighborhoods. For God's sake, they can't even come and make a simple arrest on time." I was grouchy and knew the waiting was getting on my nerves. Sam told me to be patient. I went on fussing. Vultures could be patient. Their prey had a right to complain. I was the prey and I was complaining. I was the prey of a system that sent its *finest* to clean walls instead of finding the person who killed Diana. Damn!

As if he had read my thoughts, Sam smiled and said in a light-hearted tone, "But they clean the walls so nicely."

I chuckled in spite of my anger.

"Are you trying to defuse my temper?" I asked accusingly.

"As a matter of fact ... Anyway, this is to our advantage. Chris should be out of court by noon. We really want him here for the whole show." Sam went back to his stack of work.

I knew he was right, but I just wanted to be mad. I felt like I owed it to myself. I went about emptying the trash cans - for the second time. I wanted to be angry. What had Harriet's lawyer called me? Spoiled? Well maybe. And thinking of that shyster did the trick - it made me angry!

Taravella showed up at half past noon and told us there had been a multiple murder this morning and Kisselberg was busy.

At my questioning glance, he smiled, "I have a few friends on the police force." I was a little shocked. He was so much an individualist, so thorough, so professional. I just never thought of him as having friends. He just seemed too immersed in his practice to squander time on friendships. I was sure the folks at the police station were more on the order of professional acquaintances. But, surely, Chris Taravella had friends. It was an interesting thought and a short diversion. It was almost like when you discover your parents are real people, not just Mother, and Father.

My desire for anger hadn't totally died away. But something about Taravella's presence made me more reluctant to display it. "Chris, why did the cops curtail Kisselberg's vacation and decide to arrest me today?"

"Diana's autopsy was done by one of the assistant MEs. Dr. Carpenter got back from his vacation last week and reviewed every case handled by his assistants. When he reviewed Diana's autopsy, he said the strangulation was done by someone with Special Forces training," Taravella said.

"How the hell could he know that?" I snapped.

Taravella patted my hand. "Carpenter used to be a green beret and said the method of strangulation matched a technique he'd been taught. Besides that, the mayor is in a snit because the cops haven't made an arrest in the case. John, haste makes waste. They are now in a big hurry and that works in our favor. Relax."

Of course, I couldn't relax, but Sam talked me down off the ledge.

The afternoon dragged on. Taravella seemed amused by my impatience. Lewis showed up at two with a briefcase full of motions he wanted Chris to look at. They were expecting Harriet to start another custody case as soon as she learned of my arrest. Chris and Troy were preparing for anything she could come up with.

I took a short nap. At least, I laid down on the bed. I was restless and irritated. I heard every tick of the clock and every endless silence between the ticks.

We all sat down together to watch the five o'clock news. The lead story was about an execution-style, triple homicide on the southside. On the screen was a small, run-down house surrounded by a mass of people. There was yellow police tape cordoning off the area around the house. The small yellow plastic strip seemed to be holding back the swell of curious on-lookers. There was the usual macabre air about the crowd. The last place on earth I wanted to be was at the scene of some grizzly crime. What drove people to want to look at the place where such an event had taken place? I suspected that had the murder occurred in the living room of any of those pushing, murmuring citizens, they would have moved out of the house rather than go back into *that room*. Yet, there they were trying to see into this room. All that kept them from their coveted view was a flimsy yellow strip of plastic marked: POLICE - DO NOT ENTER. Well, that yellow strip, along with Kisselberg and his officers kept the thrill seekers at bay.

Kisselberg was standing in front of the tape talking to an old woman. He was making notes in his little notebook. The little blue counter in the corner of the TV screen showed the time as 1:35 p.m.. It seemed strange. In all the years I had watched the news, I'd never seen anyone whom I actually knew. Strange.

The doorbell rang once.

Kisselberg came in and made his formal pronouncement. "Mr. John Noble, you are under arrest for the murder of Diana Faire.

"Sir, you have the right to ...

My head started to swim. This was really happening. Happening to me. I had stood up to meet Kisselberg but now I felt unstable. I prayed that I wouldn't faint. I had known this was coming. I'd known for three weeks that this was going to happen. For the last five days, I had really *known* - Kisselberg had told me.

I had pictured it in my mind. How Kisselberg would look, sound. I had planned how I would react, what I would say. I knew just how everything was going to happen in my mind, but now, here ... I was just like one of those naive characters I sent out into the landscapes of my books. Not the main characters; they were always wise and knowing. The naive ones were the lesser characters. They were, I thought bitterly, the weak people, the bad guys, the losers! Was I really like them? Like them, I always believed that bad things only happened to others - never to me. Those characters always dreamed of fighting and winning; never believing they could lose. They dreamed of finding the girl - maybe saving her from some evil - but surely finding her. They never gave a thought to loneliness. Was I really that shallow? That simple? I was! I had believed the murderer would be found. Maybe, even at the last minute, somebody would step up and say HALT! The confusion would unfold, the mystery would vanish and the good guy, me, would get off the hook.

The world went out of focus. I could hear Kisselberg reading me my rights. I couldn't understand the words, but I knew what was happening beyond the shimmering limits of my vision. This wasn't going as I had planned. Again I hoped I wouldn't faint.

I took a deep breath and tried to steady my nerves. I could hear Kisselberg's voice. No! It wasn't Kisselberg; it was Taravella. I missed the first part of what he had to say. When the world stopped rolling in front of my eyes, I heard Taravella saying, "Lieutenant, my client understands his rights. He doesn't want to make a statement or answer any questions at this time."

Kisselberg told us I'd have to ride down to police head-quarters with him. Taravella argued the point. There were two uniformed police officers with Kisselberg, so Taravella didn't mention that we knew of the arrest. He did, however, insist on me going to the police station with him. It was a short discussion of my reliability. "He's been sitting here since the murder. We have expected arrest at any moment, but Mr. Noble has been available and cooperative. He'll go with me in my car. If you prefer, Lieutenant, one of these officers can ride along."

Chris and I were alone in his car a few minutes later. I was wearing a jogging suit. Chris had planned my wardrobe - no pockets, no strings, nothing to hurt myself with, therefore nothing for the police to take from me when I was booked.

"You'll have to spend the night in jail, John. There's no way I can get you out tonight because the arrest came so late in the day. I've already talked to a judge and all the paperwork is ready. As soon as the courthouse opens in the morning, I'll have the order to release you. I should be at the jail by nine, or so. Just hang in there."

Thirty minutes after I walked into the police station, I was in a cell. Simple as that. Quick as that. Taravella gave me some last minute instructions. Don't answer any questions, whatsoever. Keep to myself. Keep my spirits up. He would be back in fourteen hours. Then he was gone and I was alone.

I was alone. I was in jail. I was charged with murder. I was alone and in jail on a murder charge. Keep your spirits up! Alone! In jail! Murder charge! Keep your spirits up! Fourteen hours! In jail! Alone!

Alone!

It all happened so quickly. I expected it to take hours to be booked. It had taken thirty minutes. Thirty minutes for them to take my statement; fingerprint me, again; take mug shots; give me jail clothes, and slap me in a cell. Alone.

How can a bureaucracy that can drag out a parking ticket - one that you want to pay - for three months, book you for murder in thirty minutes? How? Damn!

Fourteen hours!

"Mr. Noble." It was Kisselberg speaking from far away.

Don't answer any questions.

"Is there anything you need, Mr. Noble?" He was closer, but still far away. Kisselberg. He had arrested me. He was the bad guy. The enemy. Alone. In jail. Do I need anything? Bribery? Coercion? Don't answer any questions! Alone! Keep your spirits up! In jail.

"Mr. Noble!" Louder, closer, Kisselberg was demanding. He had warned me of the arrest. He swore he believed I was innocent. He took his own time to investigate. He was the good guy. A familiar face. Not quite alone. He was just beyond those bars.

"Mr. Noble! John! Snap out of it!"

Where am I? Who is yelling at me? That man over there? Why are there bars between us? Is he in jail? Who is he?

Suddenly I remembered. Kisselberg. I jerked. My heart leapt. I was drenched in sweat. A warm flush was running down my neck, my shoulders, my back. I was shaking.

Kisselberg was talking to me in a gentle, caressing voice. I didn't know what he was saying but his voice was carefully pulling me from a soft, black void.

There was light. It was cool. I breathed deeply of the conditioned air. It was like a long drink of cold, clear water. I was better.

"Are you alright, John?"

I shook my head or thought I did and took in more of that delicious air. I smiled. What time is it? The lights were low.

"Well, Mr. Noble, it's about one AM." Had I asked? Did he just guess I didn't know? How much had I said aloud?

"I just finished my reports for today, uh, yesterday, and I thought I'd come and see how you were. The guard says you've been in sort of a stupor since seven or seven-thirty. Just sitting and staring at nothing. He says you were mumbling some, too. Are you alright now?"

I think that's what he said. I didn't know if I had been talking, or not.

Kisselberg smiled and said that I had found one way to pass time in jail. "Better get some sleep." He turned and gave me a sleepy wave as he left.

* * *

It was a picture perfect morning. The bright, hot sunshine was just what an August morning in south Texas should be like. My own jogging suit was too much for the climate but that didn't matter. I was free. Freedom, like the sunlight, was bright and shiny. I said as much to Taravella as we left the jailhouse.

"Freedom is still a long way off, John. You're out of jail. That's all!" We got into his car and drove toward the freeway. Taravella drove in silence for ten minutes. He was smiling - calculating.

I didn't interrupt his mood, whatever it was. I quickly lost myself in thoughts of my own. Was Kisselberg really at my cell last night? What kind of a trance had I been in? Was it a dream? I was so deep in trying to decipher the vision that I almost jumped when Taravella suddenly spoke. "We got lucky, John. Yesterday's triple murder was very unfortunate. Those three men, God rest their souls, did, however, provide the local papers with more than enough headlines and front page material to overshadow your arrest. Between that story and a liberal beating they've been giving the mayor for the Graffiti Task Force, the arrest of a murder suspect in a case almost a month old got lost." He smiled to himself.

His comments about us profiting from the murders made me feel a little dirty. I knew intuitively I shouldn't feel that way. There's nothing dirty about getting a break, but ...

"Sam was very worried about the publicity from my arrest," I said lamely.

"I was, too," he admitted. "It could have really hurt us." After a pause, he continued, "Don't let it bug you that yesterday's crime indirectly worked for us. It's just one link in a chain. If the crime had happened a day earlier, or a day later, or not at all, Kisselberg would have arrested you earlier and I'd have had you out in three hours with little or no press. So it doesn't matter. It just happened."

I noticed he had said crime rather than murder. He was softening reality for the sake of my tarnished conscience. I decided to let his efforts work. After all, he was right. Shit happens.

He pulled into my driveway as I finished rationalizing away my disturbed feelings.

"What are you going to do today?" he wanted to know.

"Try to shower off this grimy prison feeling, then spend the rest of the day in the pool. This bright, Texas freedomshine should do me some good." My exuberance was returning.

Taravella told me that sounded like a good plan and reminded me of our appointment the next afternoon.

Chapter 26

Time is the rider that breaks youth.

~George Herbert

Where has the time gone? It's been eleven months since Diana was murdered. In some ways it seems like eleven years; in other ways, it seems like only yesterday. Eleven months is all it has been. But that short time has been filled with unbelievable stress, turmoil, and interruptions.

Someone told me once that after twenty-one days of doing something, anything, you've formed a habit. The nature of human beings is very adaptive. We can learn to cope with all manner of discomfort and grief. My mother used to say a man could get used to anything, even hanging, if he did it long enough. I guess that's true, at least the habit-forming business anyway.

I've adjusted my life around the constraints imposed by others. I've become accustomed to the idea that I'm going to be tried for murder. I've become accustomed to spending all afternoon every Wednesday with my legal staff. I've grown used to Kisselberg calling two or three times a week to say he still believed I was innocent but that the police were no closer to solving the murder than they had been last summer.

I've learned to work around the interruptions and not fly off the handle when they happened. I'm living the Serenity Prayer. I have the courage to change what I can, but there seems so little of that. I have barely enough patience to accept what I can't change. I suppose I have the wisdom to know the difference, but that doesn't mean I like it!

I also don't like the psychological warfare Harriet has been using on the kids. She's got them convinced that I'm guilty. They're suffering from her insanity and I can't do much of anything about it. I've still got my visitation rights and have worked out a comfortable way of keeping the kids too busy to consider the crap their mother tells them. At first, they were curious and asked an endless string of questions. To my credit, I answered all of their questions honestly. I guess that worked because now they seem to have put it out of their minds when their mother will let that happen.

Noel is still in town and still investigating Diana's murder but she's not coming up with anything. I think she's dropping her bucket down a dry well, as Kisselberg would say.

Noel can only see the evil step-sisters as responsible. What changed her viewpoint, I don't know, but she's after them with a vengeance. Maybe she doesn't think they actually killed Diana, but they are her obsession. Somehow, I don't think they are the ones. I can't say why; it's just a feeling.

They left San Antonio shortly after they came to my house the second time. I haven't seen them since. Thank goodness for small blessings.

Dru and Lu sent a team of lawyers down here who filed a cascade of civil suits against me. They were trying to get the death clause overturned by claiming I had murdered Diana for profit. They cited some law passed a few years ago to prevent convicted criminals from profiting from book and movie sales about the crimes they were convicted of. I think the law came up after the "Son of Sam" killings on the east coast.

That contention was quickly turned aside. Taravella easily convinced the judge and jury that Diana's murder wasn't even remotely similar to the situation covered by that law. Taravella also hammered the point that I was only accused - not convicted - of her murder.

Their next suit claimed that Diana was insane or under duress when she signed the contract. They brought out evidence that Diana had called them about the contract from my car phone. There were strong insinuations that I held a gun on her while she called. Both Higginbotham and Bayless were subpoenaed and, surprisingly, their testimony destroyed any chance the sisters may have had on that tack.

Higginbotham still hated me and probably still believed I had killed Diana, but he was eloquent in his defense of her wishes.

Just after Thanksgiving, Hoyle's publishers sent me a letter threatening to block any attempts to publish anything that even remotely touched on Hoyle's work. I'm sure the gals from out west were the driving force behind that publisher's action.

My own publisher, however, was a different story. They still haven't begun publication of my latest mystery. They had signed the contract with me but stopped working on the book when all of this mess started. They acted like there was something to gain from seeming chagrined by foul play - *suspected* foul play, I mean.

I was furious with them; Chucky was livid. We argued, asked, demanded, and threatened but all to no avail. The publisher simply stood by its decision as a profit-oriented reshuffling of priorities. That was a load of manure and everybody knew it.

"They're within their legal rights, according to the contract." Chucky had told me. "It's dirty pool, John. But they can get by with it for a little while." That was almost a year ago and I still don't know what a "little while" means.

I was adamant about withdrawing the manuscript and selling it to another publisher. Chucky was afraid that the litigation would simply delay things more. I didn't care and told him so.

Taravella, with Sam at his side, told me to let it alone for now. "We are starting to smooth things out here and a legal battle with the publishers would only muddy the waters in the murder trial."

Chucky had gotten to him. Damn!

Sam agreed with Chris and it did no good to argue with either one of them. Arguing with Taravella was annoying; he never seemed to argue back, yet you came to the conclusion that he had beaten you. He did agree, however, to write a threatening letter to Hoyle's publisher.

The way it looks to me I've been punished because I've been accused. I've had to fight for my civil rights on every front. What happened to "innocent 'til proven guilty?" Come to think of it, what happened to the guarantee of "a speedy trial?"

Noel wasn't coming up with anything new. Neither was Matt Brown. The police weren't even trying anymore. Kisselberg? Who knew what that old cowboy was up to.

If no one could turn up any more solid evidence, either to clear me or to convict me, why the delay? Of course, I knew the answer to that: lawyers! Taravella and the District Attorney were jockeying for position and advantage.

Troy Lewis was, I had to admit, worthy of the trust Sam placed in him. I had even learned to trust his unorthodox approach to legal matters. If not trust them, then at least follow blindly because he always seemed to get the desired results.

As soon as Chris told me when we would go to court, I called Lewis and told him to get my summer visitation changed to coincide with the expected trial dates. I arranged for the kids to spend that time with my parents. I was assuming that there would be no further delays since we had a firm court date. It was a chancy assumption, yet it was all I had to work with.

Lewis not only got the court to agree, but he also made all of the travel arrangements. He told me the airline tickets were the theatrical point that sold the judge. Harriet's lawyer didn't like the arrangement for the twins. But that shyster disliked whatever he was paid to dislike. Lewis impressed the judge with the plan as being in the best interests of the children. It was and the judge finally agreed.

Taravella said the trial would start soon. Soon. A speedy trial. Innocent until proven guilty. A little while. All phrases which defied definition. Or worse yet, were unlimited in the number of definitions they held.

Jury selection would begin next week. That would be a relief, but it would also be an interruption. Since I'd started on the work using Hoyle's characters, I'd become fascinated with it. I'd done nothing else.

Eleven months of grueling work had yielded a fantastic trilogy of Westerns. Chucky had questioned my judgment. "Leave it alone," he cautioned. "You may not even get the rights. Then all of your work would be wasted." Sam warned me also that I may be wasting my time. "Even once you're cleared of the murder charge, John, those Arizona women can hold this up in litigation for years. They have the money to waste and more than enough hatred to fuel their contrary deeds."

I turned a deaf ear on both of them. I was doing what I loved. I was doing it superbly. And I was extremely happy during the few uninterrupted hours of work I had each week.

I had wondered at an early stage if I was working to fulfill Diana's wish. Maybe I was building a monument to her. It seemed a crazy idea, but it stayed with me. I couldn't come up with a definitive answer, so I decided it just didn't matter. I was happy!

Now as I neared completion of the trilogy, I was going back to court. My days and nights were going to get switched around again. Damn!

But that was next week ...

Chapter 27

What takes the child by the hand takes the mother by the heart.

~German proverb

"I wish you would let your father and I stay here. You'll need some moral support, John!" At fifty-five, my mother was as spirited and stubborn as she had ever been. She was a prim, five foot one, hundred-pound wildcat who could talk a train off the tracks.

She couldn't understand my confidence in Taravella. She refused to understand. She had never met him, but that made no difference to her. She was still mad that I hadn't used her Georgia lawyers. She and Father had retained the firm of Garfield and Hill for twenty years or more. Father had told me confidentially that their lawyers had given them the highest praise for Chris. Mother had pooh-poohed their report. They were familiar to her and in her opinion, they were the best. I'd learned very young that the only opinion Mother paid any attention to was her own.

"Mother, let's have a peaceful Sunday breakfast. You and the kids are flying to Atlanta this afternoon." I did my best to put finality into the statement. That was a hard thing to do when you were dealing with my mother.

"Peaceful?" She was a little confused by my request. She had been demanding her own way for so long that it was just second nature to her. Her seemingly continuous arguing for her point was just the way she was. I don't think she even realized she could be rather disquieting.

She smiled her little smile that said so much more than words. It said I was young and innocent and naive and would understand when I grew up. That smile had worked so well when I was ten, or even twenty, and she had always gotten her way back then.

"No! Mother. You've got the tickets and it's off to Atlanta with you and the twins this afternoon." I was stern.

"You're as pigheaded as your father!" She gave up in disgust.

The children, bless their timing, came running into the kitchen just then. My dear, demanding, over-protective mother melted away to be replaced by a doting, indulgent grandmother.

She loved me as much as I loved her. She only wanted to save me, to protect me. A part of me wanted to be saved and protected, but the twins needed to be out of town during the trial. I'd taught them the social importance of reading the newspaper. They generally fulfilled their obligation with the TV listings and the funny page. Yet, if there was newsprint about the trial, Harriet would be sure they read it - especially if it was bad.

My parents would spoil the kids rotten in a month, but that's what grandparents are for, I guess. At least, the kids would be loved and protected. And, in a way, so would I.

At the appointed time, I loaded everyone's luggage into the Cadillac. A proper Southern woman, such as my mother, wouldn't ride in a pick-up truck. I wondered if I wouldn't need the truck for all of the luggage.

I wouldn't let Andrew and Amanda fly alone; I didn't think it was safe. Also, the thought of 'those two little darlings all alone, in that big old airplane' would have driven Mother crazy. She came in on Friday for the weekend and to fly back with the kids.

When she arrived she only had one suitcase - and an overnight case, of course. Now there were seven suitcases,

Mother's overnight case, and two small carry-on bags. These last two were filled with games, toys, books, and every imaginable kind of entertainment for the twins. Knowing Mother, there was probably enough entertainment for a large Cub Scout troop on a weekend campout.

She had insisted on doing the packing for the twins. She declared that men just didn't know how to pack for kids, or for anyone else, for that matter. "Your father would have gone on his business trips without even a toothbrush if I hadn't packed for him!" I had heard that same charge ever since I was twelve. Poor Father.

I was loading the car and wondering if she had packed the beds and dressers. Three suitcases for each child seemed extravagant for one month, but not to Mother.

The trip to the airport was quick and happy. The children were so excited about their vacation that Mother and I could barely restrain them. "They're pretty wound up, Mother. You're going to have your hands full."

"Why they're little darlings, John. Just don't you worry about us." In her typical fashion, she could handle anything, and she was as excited about the kids' vacation as they were.

After the appropriate hugs and kisses, they boarded the plane and I drove home. With my children safely out of harm's way, I could relax some.

Some! It all starts tomorrow.

Chapter 28

A jury consists of twelve persons chosen to decide who has the better lawyer.

~Robert Frost

Jury selection was a seemingly endless, tiring affair. The first morning proved interesting only because Chris asked the first juror if she was divorced. That set off a morning-long debate between the lawyers.

The District Attorney, a short, white-haired man named Joe Perkins, objected to the question and declared it to be irrelevant. I didn't truly understand the significance of the issue. Yet, Taravella was adamant, and once you hired him you let him do things his own way. Sam had told me that the DA had a long record of losing to Taravella. I wondered if Chris was simply trying to beat the DA on this issue to establish domain - or dominance

"Your Honor." Chris picked up one of the two dozen manila folders he had placed on the corner of our table. "Your Honor, in the case of Michigan versus Chavez, the lower court had refused to let marital status be an issue in jury selection. Chavez was convicted. Michigan Appeals Court overturned the verdict solely on that one issue."

Taravella walked over and dropped the folder on the DA's table. Picking up the second folder, Chris went on to explain that a similar situation had occurred in California.

By the time the second folder dropped on his table, Perkins was ready to argue. He had read the highlights of the Chavez trial. Chavez had been tried for killing his wife. The DA argued that, since Diana and I hadn't been married, there was no similarity between that trial and this one.

Taravella, with his third folder, pointed out that in both cases the precedent was clear. "The higher courts have all agreed that marital status, in today's society, impacts the Constitutional guarantee of a trial by *peers*. Furthermore, Your Honor, in Georgia versus Tunstall, the defendant and the victim were unrelated." He waved the folder he was holding. Chris was impressive on his battlefield with his manila battle flag.

The DA was losing the battle and could feel it. As insignificant as the issue seemed to me, losing on this point seemed very threatening to Joe Perkins.

"Your Honor," Perkins got up from his seat, "this issue seems to have precedent and is profoundly interesting, at least to some of us. However, Your Honor, its bearing on the case before this court is minuscule, at best. I fear we waste the court's valuable time for the entertainment of the counsel for the defense."

He was impressive; I held my breath waiting to hear Chris Taravella counter. I wondered how Chris would attack the insult he had received.

"Your Honor, the case against my client is largely circumstantial. Circumstances of violent behavior by Mr. Noble are the chassis for Mr. Perkins' case. Mr. Noble does have a few incidents of violence in his past. However, Your Honor, the key issues that Mr. Perkins plans to present as evidence center around incidents which occurred during Mr. Noble's long, bitter, troubled divorce."

Taravella had moved around behind me as he spoke. He gently put his hands on my shoulders and quietly went on. "Your Honor, for Mr. Noble to get a fair trial by a jury of *his* peers, we intend to show that those acts that the District Attorney calls unwarranted violence were reactions to the circumstances of Mr. Noble's life at the time. We concede, Your Honor, that they were excessive reactions, but not traits inherent in the defendant's normal lifestyle. Or traits indicative of a murderer."

He was still resting his hands on my shoulders, presenting the guardian-angel image. "Your Honor, in the interest of justice, the jurors must know, first hand, some of the unsettling emotions of the trauma of divorce. That is, in fact, the only way we ensure that the members of the panel are Mr. Noble's peers."

In the silence following Chris' appeal, I noticed Perkins had already sat down, accepting the defeat and aiding it by his actions.

"Mr. Taravella, I will allow this line of inquiry, however, I will *not* dismiss someone only on the basis of not having been divorced." Her Honor dismissed the court for a two-hour recess.

Chris Taravella was the winner in the first battle and proved to be a gracious winner. For his part, Perkins accepted the defeat with ease. The two men chatted briefly, amicably, before departing for lunch.

That afternoon, the DA eliminated a lady because she said she loved my books. Chris got rid of a fellow who thought I'd been very creative in one of my mystery novels - a murder mystery. All in all, I was getting a lot of local publicity, or exposure. I didn't want any of it. I never had and I certainly did not want it now.

Sam's prophecy about the average guy hating me for trying to get ahead by murdering Diana was coming to pass. That seemed to be a common sentiment among many of the prospective jurors. Chris Taravella sent all of those who thought that way out of the courtroom. By the end of the first week, we had nine jurors. The last three took another week. Sam told me he had never seen a trial where empanelment had taken more than two days.

One well-dressed young businessman got on the stand and the judge asked if he had formed an opinion about the case to be tried. The fellow smiled a little and said, "No. Let's give the guilty bastard a fair trial and then hang him." The judge wasn't amused; she fined the young businessman for contempt and sent him on his way.

Taravella whispered, "That fellow just didn't want to be on a jury. Shirking his civic duty cost him a fine, but he'll be back at work in an hour." He took a totally different attitude with the judge. Chris argued eloquently that the statement was a general trend in San Antonio. "We must, for the rights of the innocent, Your Honor, change the venue. Time and public opinion are such that my client can not possibly get a fair trial here in San Antonio." Chris took a motion from his briefcase.

Her Honor smiled. "Your motion is on file, Mr. Taravella, We've had our pre-trial hearing on the matter. The trial stays here." It wasn't the first time he had filed a motion to get the trial moved. The judge denied this request just as she had all of the others. The trial would be here and Taravella said privately that it was alright. He explained that he was just laying the groundwork for an appeal, if it came to that.

Lawyers!

The final jury consisted of nine men and three women. Six of the men and one woman were divorcees. There was a journalist, a freelance writer, and two business owners. Eight of the dozen said they had read some of my work or had at least heard of it - no haters and no die-hard fans.

I wondered how, with eleven, no ten, of my novels in print, four of these people could have never heard of me. My ego was a little pierced!

Chapter 29

Everyone is a prisoner of his own experiences.

~*Edward R. Murrow*

The jury selection had been generally boring. It had an impact on my life so I tried to stay interested and almost succeeded. Choosing the twelve people who would decide my fate had been a battle of wits and wills between Taravella and Perkins. There were surprisingly few references, direct or indirect, to me or the murder.

The trial was vastly different! The first morning was slow. All of the administrative procedures dragged on 'til nearly lunch.

As soon as Her Honor took her seat after the midday break, Perkins launched into his opening statement. It was quite an oration extolling all of the evils, greed, weakness, and loathsome characteristics of my life. That was rough. Sam kept passing me notes telling me to chill out. He drew smiling faces on some of them, caricatures on others. He and Chris had forewarned me of how intimidating this part of the process would be, yet their earnest warnings hadn't prepared me in the least.

At the end of the humiliating ordeal, Sam pushed me a note. It simply said, 'That took seventeen minutes.' Astonished, I checked my watch. He was right; I'd have sworn Perkins had been at it for hours. When I looked back, Sam smiled and pushed me another note. It was an amazingly lifelike caricature of Perkins complete with horns, tail, and cloven hooves. I was impressed with Sam's artistic talent.

Chris had stood as soon as Perkins stopped talking. He stood silently inspecting the jury. After a very pregnant pause, he began his opening remarks. His comments were not a flowery praise to offset the blunt, hard words the panel had already heard.

There was a measured honest quality in his words, power in his voice. He carefully reminded the twelve that they had each made mistakes in there past. Those past faults had, hopefully, been forgiven and forgotten. A couple of members of the panel shifted self-consciously in their seats like they were recalling the errors Chris had alluded to. I thought of the Bible story where Jesus wrote something in the dirt and each person thought He had written about them.

Chris continued saying he was sure all of the jury members had learned from whatever mistakes they had been guilty of making. He was speaking to twelve people all at once but the words he used made his speech a one-on-one conversation. Each member of the panel could, and probably did, feel Chris Taravella was speaking directly to him or her alone.

"Mr. Noble has made mistakes, too. And like you, like me, he has learned from his mistakes. He, like you and I, has paid for his errors, learned from them, and become a better person because of them."

Leaning on the banister that defined the jury's space, Chris continued softly, "His mistakes are not the trademarks of a murderous demon as Mr. Perkins would have you believe. They were mistakes, Ladies and Gentlemen, just that! Mr. Perkins wants you to believe that because of certain events in the defendants past, events in no way connected to this case, that Mr. Noble is a cold-blooded murderer. Mr. Perkins wants you to believe that, because he can not prove that John Noble did, in fact, murder Diana Faire.

"Mr. Perkins can't prove that, Ladies and Gentlemen of the Jury, because it simply isn't true! John Noble did not commit any crime and certainly not the crime for which he is being tried.

"Her Honor has already told you your duty is to listen to the facts surrounding the murder and decide Mr. Noble's guilt or innocence. Mr. Perkins is responsible to prove to you, beyond the shadow of a doubt, that John Noble is guilty of murdering Diana Faire. Mr. Perkins must prove to you that the defendant is guilty of murder, not that he's guilty of those unrelated mistakes he made before! You must listen carefully and then more carefully decide if each bit of information is a fact or a non-fact. Proof comes with facts, not with circumstances or insinuations.

"Beyond the shadow of a doubt, you must have proof, facts, that John Noble is guilty of something he did not do!"

Chris' twenty-four-minute opening statement did a lot to relieve my floundering spirit. Sam gave me a drawing of Taravella with a halo and wings - and a happy face.

It was Wednesday of the following week before Perkins was ready to call his final witness. Harriet was to be the prosecution's *coup-de-gras*. The state's case was substantially loaded with circumstantial evidence - more than enough to prove I'd been violent. Yet upon cross-examination, Chris had shown the violence to be a reaction to the situation. He clearly showed that when I'd been violent, it was as a last resort.

I wasn't very proud of my past. It was laid naked before the world and I found much to be ashamed of.

Perkins had shown that I'd had the opportunity to kill Diana. With Tuttle, the Arizona copyright lawyer who had worked for Diana, on the stand, Perkins had also claimed that I had a motive: the death clause giving me all of Hoyle's copyrights. However, Chris heatedly contested the point on motive.

"Is it not true, Mr. Tuttle, that according to the terms of the contract, Mr. Noble had exclusive use of those copyrights?" Tuttle agreed and Chris went on. "Is it not also true that Mr. Noble had very little, if anything at all, to gain from owning the copyrights outright?"

"There would have been some additional royalties if Mr. Noble owned everything. But it wouldn't have come to much compared with continuing the work Mr. Hoyle had started."

"So, Mr. Tuttle, you're saying my client had no reason to kill Mrs. Faire?"

"Objection!" Perkins shot out of his chair. "Calls for a conclusion on the part of the witness."

Taravella withdrew the question without waiting for the objection to be ruled on. "Mr. Tuttle, it is safe to say, based on your vast experience, that Mr. Noble had very little to gain financially from Mrs. Faire's death." Tuttle nodded.

"Then since my client is a very wealthy man, the terms of the contract offer no incentive to murder. Do they Mr. Tuttle?"

"Objection! Your Honor the witness is in no position to testify about Mr. Noble's financial status. Counsel is leading the witness." Perkins was standing again.

"Sustained. The last question and the answer will be stricken from the record. And," consulting her watch, "this court is in recess until one o'clock this afternoon."

Chapter 30

Where there are no tigers, a wildcat is very self-important.

~Korean proverb

The courtroom seemed a little brighter. Taravella sat in the trance-like state he always assumed when the District Attorney was questioning a witness. Harriet sat in the witness chair, her back straight, hands folded in her lap. The DA was plying her with questions about my violent past. Her answers were clear and immediate. She was obviously nervous but seemed to be enjoying herself and her well-rehearsed testimony.

Kisselberg leaned over the rail and nudged Sam. The policeman's face was split with a victorious grin and he winked at me. He thrust a note into Sam's hand and scurried out of the courtroom.

Sam looked at me and shrugged. He spread the note on the table before us. Scrawled on a crumpled page ripped from Kisselberg's notebook, was a simple message: I found the fly in the ointment! Stop the trial.

"What does the Lieutenant mean about a fly in the ointment?" Sam whispered to me.

"It's his way of saying there's something out of place. I guess he thinks he's found it."

"Let's hope he's right. If Chris stops the trial without good cause, Her Honor will kill him." He pushed Kisselberg's note over to me and motioned toward Taravella.

I slid the note toward Chris and put my hand on his arm. I wasn't sure he knew I was even at the table. He was absorbing everything that went on. I put a little pressure on his arm to get his attention.

His wrist pivoted and his hand came up with the fingers spread. I'd seen the signal before; he knew I was trying to get his attention but his concentration was on Harriet and the DA. He moved his hand toward me slightly and without looking covered Kisselberg's note. He slid it in front of his tie.

Chris Taravella bewildered me. He knew, or was aware of, everything happening in the courtroom. His brain seemed to process all of the information at once and catalog it instantly. He still sat staring; his eyes boring into the space between the DA and the witness.

Taravella glanced quickly at the note as the DA announced, "No further questions, Your Honor." Looking up from the note, Chris Taravella locked his gaze on Harriet for a long moment. Harriet's prim, happy attitude wilted under that intense stare. She was sure the cross-examination wasn't going to be nearly as much fun as her earlier testimony had been. Lawyers aren't allowed to badger a witness, but Taravella had just done so with his eyes. "I have no questions for the witness at this time, Your Honor."

The judge dismissed Harriet and consulted the clock on the back wall of the courtroom. "Court will recess until 9:00 AM, tomorrow," she announced and rapped her gavel.

The bailiff ordered all to rise and the judge left the room. The rest of the court clearing ritual, with its attendant cacophony of noise, began as the door to 'chambers' closed behind the judge.

"We were fortunate, John. I don't know why Her Honor quit early today, but she seldom delays a trial at the request of the defense." He was carefully packing his briefcase while Sam and I were cramming notepads into ours. As we turned toward the spindle fence that separated us from the pews where the newspeople and the general public sat, Chris added, "Both of you meet me in my office at 7:00 p.m. Eat before you get there; it may be a long night. And, if you see Kisselberg, tell him to be there, too."

Sam knew what was coming as well as I did. Taravella would go over every word spoken in the courtroom that day. He'd ply us with questions of every description about what was said, how it was said, what it was related to, and what our feelings were about all of it. Some of these sessions got pretty spirited when we'd heard something differently or attached a different meaning to it.

He would watch our reactions and expressions. He would leap on anything that might provide a different twist or insight on the case, no matter how trivial it seemed.

Hiring Taravella was a unique experience. He worked us hard, relentlessly hard. Kisselberg, in his official capacity, on his own time, was still committed to proving my innocence. By doing so, he exposed himself to Taravella's work ethic. The cop had been quickly and definitely drawn into the meetings, discussions, and general defense.

I had questioned Sam on the ethics of the arresting officer being so intimately involved in the case. He said that was Taravella's business. "Chris is good," Sam had emphasized, "really good and he's got a great reputation. He can get away with things other lawyers would go to jail for. He gets by with it just because of who he is."

Chapter 31

Madness is a part of us all, all the time, and it comes and goes, waxes and wanes.

~*Otto Freidrich*

Court had been called into session and the judge motioned for Taravella to proceed. The DA interrupted and asked to make a statement. He stood up, cleared his throat, and informed the court that his office was dropping all charges against me.

Kisselberg came into the courtroom as the judge was questioning the DA's motion. Kisselberg was wearing that same victory grin he'd had when he rushed out of the courtroom the afternoon before.

The DA explained that the real murderer had been arrested and had confessed to the crime. "She confessed and provided a full statement, with her attorney present. Her statement completely exonerates the defendant, Your Honor." He turned to face me and went on, "The District Attorney's Office would like to apologize to the defendant for any inconvenience he may have suffered."

I was so stunned I barely heard the judge say I was free to go and the case was dismissed.

Sam was pumping my hand and talking to me but I couldn't tell what he was saying. Kisselberg leaned over the rail and shook my shoulder. The present surroundings came back to me with a terrifying rush.

"John, I can imagine your confusion. Lieutenant Kisselberg can explain this better than I can. Let's find an empty room somewhere." Taravella's voice showed none of the excitement of winning - only the professionalism it always held. Of course, he didn't win but I don't think he would have shown any emotion if he had.

There was an empty jury deliberation room just down the hall from the courtroom. We all went in there: Taravella, Kisselberg, Sam, and I. Troy Lewis showed up from somewhere and joined us.

The room was brightly lit with one long table in the middle of the room. Everyone dropped into a chair except Kisselberg. Almost everyone was wearing a big bright smile. For my part, I was still bewildered.

Kisselberg, ignoring the prominent 'No Smoking' sign on the wall, sat on the edge of the table and lit up. "I found the fly in the ointment." His smile was electric and contagious. I felt myself smiling back at him and heard myself asking him to explain.

The lieutenant couldn't tell things straight out. He had to build a background of words so everyone was sure to see why his story was correct. I'd been irritated by this habit of his over the past months; now it was a blessing. As he went through the preliminaries, I returned, mentally, to the present. I was free. The charges had been dropped. Someone else was guilty and I could get back to living my life.

I looked around the little room and thought of some old TV series about a lawyer. This was almost like the end of most of those shows. Everyone sitting around listening to an explanation of how everything fits together and how the hero solved the mystery. Only it wasn't the lawyer-hero character doing the explaining, or even the lawyer's private investigator character.

It was Kisselberg!

"Last month, I started over from scratch. There were just too many facts and they were all attached to the working theory

that you killed Ms. Faire. If you put too many lights and decorations on a Christmas tree, you can't tell if the tree is straight or not. You really have to check it when it's bare."

I stifled a groan.

"Well, anyway, I started over, and like I told you the first time I met you, John, I figured you were innocent. Somebody else killed the girl and tried to frame you.

"Now that makes two Christmas trees, two separate theories. So I had to work them one at a time. I investigate murders for a living, so I started with the question of who killed the girl.

"Nobody but her sisters really wanted her dead and they came out losing because of the contract you signed over her daddy's copyrights. Every other suspect led me down a blind alley. I had suspected the woman I arrested last night - but she had no motive. At least, none that I could see. Another blind alley."

"Who is she?" I asked.

Kisselberg dropped his burned-out cigarette on the chocolate and white tile floor and stepped on it. "Since I couldn't figure out who did the killing, I had to try to figure out who was framing you. If I could break that mystery, I could work backward to find the right person to arrest for murder.

"What didn't fit was the intimacy of the details. The killer, whoever it turned out to be, was someone who knew you and your lifestyle very well. There didn't seem to be anyone pushing the evidence in our faces. Whoever set up this frame was very sneaky. Ms. Faire's sisters had plenty of reason to frame you so they could get those copyrights back. But they couldn't control all of the evidence. Besides, they ain't sneaky; they rush in like a bull in a china shop. There wasn't anybody else. Just nobody."

Kisselberg lit another cigarette and went on. I think he sensed my frustration with his twisted chain of logic. "Mr. Noble, nobody was framing you! It just sort of worked out that way. All of the pieces fell into place and the killer just let everything alone at first. It worried her some after that. Then she'd push the frame, then she would lay off or even retract some of it. When I first questioned her, she swore you didn't kill the girl. That should have tipped me off, but I missed the subtlety of it. Sorry."

"Damnit, Kisselberg! Get on with the story!" I screamed.

"John," the cop said quietly, "believe it or not, in her own twisted way, your ex-wife still loves you. She killed that girl in a jealous rage."

I just stared at him.

"Harriet?"

"Yes, John. Harriet Noble strangled Diana Faire to death in a fit of passionate jealousy."

My hands were shaking as I pulled the cigarette pack out of Kisselberg's shirt pocket. "Your long-winded explanations are hard on all of us, Kisselberg, but you had better go ahead and fill in the gaps."

The homicide detective continued his tale. "The fly in the ointment, Mr. Noble, was the restraining order, the first one, keeping you from seeing your kids." Kisselberg waited with smug satisfaction as the looks of confusion grew.

He could see I wasn't making the connection, so he went on in the same smug fashion. "Anyway, as I was saying about that restraining order, do you remember when they served it on you?"

Everything back then was just a blur, a hazy memory that wouldn't focus. "No, not really. Is that important?"

Instead of answering me, he posed the same question to Troy Lewis. Troy recited the date.

"That's right. Friday, July tenth. Miss Faire's body was discovered on the ninth, Thursday the ninth." Again Kisselberg waited for us to grasp the significance of these facts. Lewis' face showed he understood, yet the rest of us needed to be spoon-fed.

"I went to the court records office, yesterday. The motion for the restraining order was filed with the presiding judge at two o'clock in the afternoon on Thursday the ninth. There was nothing connecting you with the Jane Doe until you identified her body at about that same time. Mrs. Noble's attorney had to draw up the paperwork and present it to the court. At the time the lawyer started doing the paperwork, the only one who knew who the dead girl was and that you were in any way connected to her, was the killer."

It all made sense; the part of how the police solved it made sense. Why had Harriet killed Diana? How had she done it? None of that made any sense.

"It seems that Mrs. Noble had gone to the airport on Wednesday, July eighth." Kisselberg's saga wasn't at an end yet. "She went to drop off a friend, or so she said. Anyway, while she was there, she saw Ms. Faire in the parking lot. Your ex said she recognized your cowboy hat. I haven't seen that hat, John, but when I get back to the station, I'm going to the evidence room to take a look. It must be something special if Mrs. Noble could recognize it across the airport parking lot."

Sam and I exchanged glances.

"Anyway, she says this hat was a present to you or something like that. And she saw this other woman wearing it and getting into your truck alone. She also said something about you never let her drive your truck. That seems a pretty petty thing to me, but your ex-wife was really bent out of shape about it. Anyway, she followed the truck. Ms. Faire went to her hotel. Mrs.

Noble pulled right up beside her and got into the truck. They struggled and in the scuffle, she killed Ms. Faire. Did it right there in the parking lot of a ritzy hotel in broad daylight." He shook his head in true amazement.

"Then Mrs. Noble got scared and drove the truck, with the body in the passenger's seat, out of the hotel parking lot. According to her, she decided to hide the body somewhere and drove around for a couple of hours in a panic trying to think. She said the only place she could think of to dump the body was your RV lot. She took most of the clothes off the dead girl and emptied her pockets. She was trying to make it look like robbery or rape or something other than what it was. Trying to throw suspicion off her trail - and yours. That woman is really mixed up. I'm no shrink or anything, but I'd say she's schizo.

"Well, she almost emptied the pockets - she missed the scrap of paper with your phone number on it.

"She said she was afraid you'd get blamed if your truck was found near the body, so she took it to your house. It was around ten and already dark. She knew you'd be asleep and so she just parked the truck in your driveway, walked down to the supermarket, called a cab, and went to get her car."

"Early the next morning her insanity took a different path; she figured this would be a good chance to get the twins away from you for good. She called her lawyer and got him started on that restraining order. He didn't know that the body hadn't been identified or anything. He just did his thing on the custody issue as his client instructed."

I interrupted. "But if she covered it up so I wouldn't be suspected, then how could she figure to use it against me?"

"John, like I said, your ex-wife is a mighty mixed up lady. She said her sanity had come back the next day, Thursday, but that's questionable. I don't think it has ever come back. She really didn't want you to get convicted, but she wanted to hurt you by taking the kids away from you. She kept demanding to know how you could let some, ah, other woman, wear your hat and drive your truck. She's really screwed up. Hates you one minute, loves you the next."

I'd have to try to sort that out later.

I told the assembled members of my little band that I had to go. Taravella said it was a tragedy that Diana had fought real danger for so long and then, just when she was safe, for something like this to happen. Lewis said he had gotten a call from Kisselberg late the evening before. "When he told me of your ex's arrest and confession, I drew up the paperwork for you to have sole custody of the children. Harriet is going to beat the murder rap with an insanity plea. I'm very sure of that, but she'll be in institutions for a very, very long time. You've got permanent custody. You'll probably have to let the kids go see their grandparents, Harriet's folks, for a little while in the summers but everything else is in your hands. That's what I've been doing down here this morning."

I stamped out my cigarette on the floor beside Kisselberg's. I was in a state of shock. Harriet had killed Diana. I was free. I had the kids. The kids were safe - or were they? They would need a lot of help. Mother could help. I needed to call her.

I grabbed my head and tried to stop the world from spinning so rapidly. Sam rested a hand on my shoulder. "Take your time, John. The kids will still be with your parents for another week. You've got a lot to do, but you've got a lot of time to do it. Those kids will need a lot of help from you to get over this. They've already been through a lot and there's more to come. I'll call you later and leave you the number of a good psychologist."

Taravella and Lewis left while I was trying to grasp the rapid changes that had happened in my life - and the changes yet to come. I could no longer be the night-owl. The temporary schedule changes I had forced upon myself two or three week-ends a month now had to become a permanent change. I'd have to learn to write in the daytime. Could I do that? I had the twins and their well being to consider so, of course, I could do anything that I needed to do.

I looked around and Kisselberg smiled. He pulled a ciga-rette out of his pocket and shook the pack at me. "No thanks, Lieutenant. I quit smoking five years ago. It's time to quit again. The kids will be in the house and I don't want them to learn bad habits from me."

"There's that and second-hand smoke, John. You're mak-ing a good decision." He stuck the pack and his unlit cigarette back in his pocket. "I wish I could quit the damned things. Maybe when I retire."

Sam said, "Sometimes a lifestyle change can help. Right, John!"

"My life has sure changed in the last hour," I agreed.

"And there's more to come. Much more, John. You're go-ing to turn into a respectable, daytime citizen."

I looked at him quizzically. "You say that like it's bad, Sam."

"Oh, no! Not bad at all, just different. I've known you for a long time and you've always been quite a character. Your legal business was never mundane. I'm going to miss that flare, but I welcome the change."

"A character?" I asked.

"Quite a character. But the impending changes in your life will assassinate that character. You'll be much better off for it and so will your kids and the other people that are in your life."

He was right; I knew he was and a restless something in me died right there in that jury room. Kisselberg left promising to come by my house later. I didn't hold any feelings of intrusion about his coming.

Sam quickly outlined the rest of the things the others had done to get my life started on its new track.

Everything seemed to be falling into place. It only did so because so many people cared and went out of their way to look after the details.

Even a hermit needs people, even if people do complicate life.

About the Author

Ray Collins is an award-winning author, editor, publisher and educator. He has published Westerns, mysteries, historical fiction, sea stories, fantasies and poetry and magazine articles along with a wide variety of educational materials.

Ray has a Master's Degree in Education. He speaks to writing groups, and coaches new writers. He lives in San Antonio with his wife, Dr. Darlene D. Collins, also a published author. Together they operate a publishing firm and research their books and work as entrepreneurs, trainers, teachers, and coaches. They hike the mountains of the Land of Enchantment, and care for a large family of seven (grown) children, fourteen grandchildren (so far), and three great-grandchildren (so far).

Visit Ray at www.raydarbooks.com. He invites all to share their comments on his work.

Other Books by Ray Alan Collins

The Extinct Cowboy
Deep Canyon Rising
Freedom's Price
Contempt of Congress
Old School
The Last Manhunt
Saplings Vol I
Saplings Vol II

Other Books from RayDar Publishing

The Real Illusion of Fear – Darlene D. Collins, PhD

Visit www.raydarbooks.com for descriptions and more information on these books.

www.ingramcontent.com/pod-product-compliance
Lightning Source LLC
Chambersburg PA
CBHW071510170626
46811CB00007B/2802